DEADLY LITTLE GAMES

SARA C. ROETHLE

1

Gabriel gripped my hand where it pressed against his chest, then slowly removed it. The glow remained until his fingers slid from mine.

His dark eyes watched me with unsettling intensity. "You need to come back to the Bogs, Eva. It's the only way we can keep you safe."

I gripped my covers around me. "No way. I'm not going to be trapped there. You need to explain why you suddenly think I'm in so much danger."

His jaw clenched, his dark eyes intense. "If anyone else finds out about this, they'll want to use you. Imagine if the vampires knew you could increase their power."

"The vampires had a great time manhandling me earlier tonight." My eyes flicked to the rim of daylight beneath my blackout curtains. "Or last night, I guess. None of them started glowing."

"Perhaps it's just those of us with blood from the far realms." His eyes lifted to my bookshelf. "Come here."

It was only then that I realized Ringo had retreated from the foot of the bed to his spot on my shelf. He huddled in the little pile of pillowcases I had put there for him.

"It's okay," I said.

At my words he shifted, then hopped down from the bookshelf to scamper across the floor. He climbed up my bed toward us.

"Touch her," Gabriel ordered

Ringo extended one tiny trembling blue paw toward my arm. He placed it against my bare skin.

Nothing happened.

"See?" I said. "It's just some weird fluke thing. My magic is only reacting to Mistral, you, and Sebastian."

"Sebastian?" He reared back.

"You guys need to learn to be a little less touchy when I mention him."

He lowered his chin. "It is bad enough for him to know of these changes, but for you to react to him in this way? He will push you for more. You cannot trust him."

"Obviously." I shook my head and released my grip on my covers. "But he's going to help me, in exchange for me helping him. And I have to meet with the elf king today."

He blinked at me. "Surely you jest. Only an idiot would find all this out about herself and go marching into Emerald Heights."

"I have to go. I owe his daughter a favor."

He lifted a brow. "Princess Millelena?"

"Yeah, though she introduced herself to me as just *Elena*. She saved our cookies last night, and asked me to come speak with her father in return."

"Cookies?"

I rolled my eyes. "Yeah, you know, like our butts? The vampires kidnapped my roommate and were trying to throw him off a building."

He gripped my hand. "An even greater reason to be cautious then. You cannot go to Emerald Heights, Eva." The glow started again where our skin touched, filling my chest with a warm tingling sensation.

I wanted more of it. Every time one of them touched me and gave me this feeling, I wanted *more*.

His eyes drifted down to the glow and he yanked his hand away. "If you go to Emerald Heights, we can't protect you."

"Well good thing I don't think the elves want to hurt me. Like I said, they saved us last night."

He gave me a look like I was being very stupid. "And why do you think Princess Millelena wants you to come? If she saved you last night, then she knows about the game. She knows about the sword. Her father came from the elven realm. He is trapped here, just like Mistral. But his motivation to return to his home will be even greater."

"Why?"

His shoulders slumped. "It is only rumor, but some

say that when he came here, he left his queen behind, not knowing he would be unable to return to her."

My stomach sank. Elves were extremely long lived creatures. Who knew how long he and his queen had been together before he came here? And now to be apart, all this time. "That's awful."

"It is. But if anyone is to acquire the Realm Breaker, it will be Mistral."

I furrowed my brow. "But can't others use it too? Maybe Mistral can use it to go home, and the elf king can use it as well."

I felt a small squirming sensation in my chest at the thought of Mistral going home. It would mean never seeing him again. I had only known him a short time, but I found I didn't like the idea.

I shook my head. "Never mind. This is all conjecture. We don't even know if the sword can actually do what everyone believes. If you would have asked me a few days ago, I would have said it was a myth. So first thing first, I have to go meet with the elf king. Then Sebastian and I are going to continue searching for my mother."

Gabriel clenched his fists again at the mention of Sebastian.

"Oh no." I held up a finger. "I don't want to hear it. I have a contract with him, and you know what that means."

"You also have a bargain with Mistral. *Two* bargains."

I rolled my eyes. "Yes, I haven't forgotten. And that first bargain pertains to Sebastian. So tell Mistral I'm just fine, and I will report to him when I'm able." I gave him a look. "Unless he wants to come here himself."

His mouth sealed into a grim line. I was pretty sure by now that Mistral couldn't come here himself, and I was growing increasingly curious as to why that was.

But it was a problem for another time.

I shooed him aside so I could climb out of bed. "Now if you don't mind, I need to get dressed."

"You're being foolish, Eva." But he went for the door.

I turned to watch him reaching for the knob. "I'm half human. Foolishness is in my blood."

He hung his head, shook it, then left the room. A moment later I heard my apartment door opening and shutting.

I looked down at my hand. It seemed perfectly normal now, but the glow had been *very* real. And I had really shifted fully last night. Maybe the Realm Breaker wasn't even necessary. Maybe I could learn to shift to the near realms on my own, like a real celestial. But could I bring someone with me?

I had no idea, because my mother had left me with so little. I didn't know anything about my magic. Maybe meeting with the elf king, an ancient being with vast knowledge, could be my first step toward finding out.

2

THE DAYS WERE GETTING WARMER, but luckily not warm enough for shorts, so I ended up in black jeans, black sneakers, and a dark purple crop top. I went out to the living room, glancing toward Braxton's door. Not a single sound emanated from within.

I tiptoed toward the kitchen to make coffee, and with another glance at Braxton's door, I started searching through the cupboards for something nice to feed him when he woke up. I was still feeling guilty for getting him kidnapped by vampires, even though I knew he didn't hold it against me.

I wasn't sure what I had hoped to find, but I didn't appreciate every cupboard I opened mocking me with its emptiness. I closed the final cupboard with a sigh. Maybe a trip to the nearby café was in order.

I waited for Ringo to emerge from the bathroom, his fur damp and all fluffed up from his regular bath in the sink. He hopped over to the sofa where he started using his tiny paws to smooth down his fur.

"Mind telling Braxton not to go anywhere if he wakes up? I'll be right back."

Ringo blinked his big round eyes at me. "Is it safe?"

I patted the back pocket of my jeans where I had slid Sebastian's calling card after a short internal debate. "If anything happens, I'll summon Sebastian. By this point, I'm pretty sure he wants to keep me alive." That was, while he wasn't kissing me to summon my elusive magic.

Ringo still didn't seem convinced.

"I'll bring you a sweet potato turnover."

He sat up a little straighter. "I'll tell Braxton you'll be back soon."

Grinning, I went for the door, then hurried down the exterior stairs. It was hotter outside than I had expected, but then again, I had slept a lot of the morning away.

I reached the street and started walking, feeling on guard in an entirely new way. You always had to watch your back in the city, but the idea had gained a whole new meaning to me lately. I was sweating by the time I had traversed the few blocks to the coffee shop.

I smiled at a few familiar faces as I hurried up the sidewalk. The familiar people weren't exactly friends, but Braxton and I were regulars. We saw the other patrons pretty often.

The bells on the door jingled happily as I let myself

inside, enjoying the feel of the air conditioner. There was a line, of course, and the bakery display was mostly empty at the late hour. Once it was finally my turn, only a few things were left. Luckily one of those things was a lingonberry turnover. Braxton's favorite.

I ordered the turnover and several other pastries, along with two lattes, from the half goblin teenager behind the counter. I couldn't help but wonder if he was also reporting to Mistral. He seemed to know all the goings on within the city, even though I wasn't sure if he actually ever left the Bogs.

Pastry bag in one hand, and two lattes in a little cardboard carrier in the other, I turned to leave, nearly running into the next customer in line.

Sebastian smiled down at me as I fumbled to not spill the coffees. For once, he wasn't wearing a suit, just gray slacks and a white button up with the first few buttons left open to show the top of his chest. Maybe devils were also affected by the heat, though I doubted it. Rumor had it the hells were a realm of eternal, blistering summer.

I realized I was staring at him with my jaw hanging open and quickly averted my gaze, thinking of our kiss just the night before. "What do you want?"

He splayed his hands. "Did I not tell you I would see you today?"

I walked past him toward the door. "Not at this ungodly hour."

He followed, opening the door for me, which I

grudgingly accepted since my hands were full. "It's 1 PM."

I sighed as I walked back out into the heat. At least the coffees wouldn't get cold. "Well as you're aware, I didn't get much sleep last night."

He fell into step beside me as I walked. Insects buzzed above the din of daytime conversation and the cheerful chirping of birds.

Sebastian moved a little closer to my shoulder. "A goblin visited you early this morning."

I stopped at a crosswalk, using my elbow to push the button. "Yep."

"What did he want?"

I batted my eyelashes and gave him a fake sweet look as I waited for the light to turn. "None of your gods damned business." Except that the goblin in question had made my skin glow, just like Sebastian. He had awakened more hidden magic I didn't even know I had.

The light turned green. I hung my head and kept walking amongst a few others crossing the street. I really needed to speak with Mistral. Maybe after I visited Emerald Heights, I could escape to the Bogs for the evening. Of course, that meant leaving Braxton alone at the apartment. Elena had said the vampires wouldn't be troubling us again, but I wasn't sure if I could trust her with Braxton's life.

When we eventually reached the stairs to my apartment, Sebastian started following me up.

I turned around on the step above him, putting us at

almost eye level. "I don't remember inviting you up."

A hint of fire in his eyes made me sweat. "We need to discuss what you will say to the elf king. Elena was there last night. She may have had spies watching the roof. We cannot say if anyone saw you fully shift, but you need to be prepared should the topic arise."

My gut squirmed. Without another word, I turned and kept walking. I reached my door and went inside, hesitating for just a moment before leaving it open for Sebastian to walk in after me. Braxton was sitting inside on the sofa. I didn't see Ringo anywhere. He must have delivered his message, then retreated back to my room for a nap.

I lifted the coffees and bag of pastries, and Braxton smiled. He looked a bit rumpled in his sweats with his curly hair poking out all over the place, but he was otherwise unscathed. Werewolves were fast healers. And the smile made me feel better. He wasn't upset with me.

I would hold onto that blessing, because I was sure there weren't a lot more of them waiting in my future.

Ignoring Sebastian as he shut the door behind us, I went to sit on the sofa next to Braxton, offering him one of the coffees. I set the pastry bag on the low coffee table as Sebastian moved to lean against the nearest wall, crossing his arms.

With a smirk, Braxton moved to the floor, using the coffee table like an actual table as he took out the only lingonberry pastry and put it on a napkin.

With a smirk to match Braxton's, Sebastian took the vacated seat, sitting a little too close to me for my liking. I sensed just a touch of his dark magic, once again making me think of the previous night, of the feel of that magic crawling up my skin while his hands gripped me against him.

Braxton watched the devil, the wary look in his eyes belying his casual demeanor. "Think you can do a better job of protecting Eva today?"

Unaffected, Sebastian leaned back and crossed an ankle over his knee. "She must venture to Emerald Heights on her own, but if she'll listen to me, I can keep her out of trouble."

Braxton snorted, then took a bite of his pastry. With his mouth half full, he muttered, "You should know by now, Eva doesn't listen to anyone."

Sebastian gave me a sidelong glance. "I'm well aware, but hopefully after last night, she will change her ways. The elves have a powerful foothold in the city, and they are allied with Elizabeta, the master of all local vampires." He gave me a meaningful look. "Perhaps Ivan worked for himself, but should Elizabeta decide she wants in on the game, the elves will become our enemies."

I sulked as I sipped my latte. "All the better for me to get the meeting over with."

"Indeed," Sebastian agreed. "Learn what information you may, and tell them as little as possible."

I lifted my coffee cup in agreement, though he had

no matching vessel to cheers me with. Not that I felt guilty about that. He could have bought his own damn coffee.

I noticed Ringo peeking out of my slightly ajar door. I leaned forward, pulling out a pastry filled with purple sweet potato from the bag. I dangled it in the air, and he rushed out of the room and hopped onto my knee, holding his little paws out for the pastry. I gave it to him and he started munching away, leaving crumbs all over my jeans.

Sebastian watched Ringo with thinly-veiled disgust. "Do you plan on keeping that thing forever?"

I pulled the pastry bag next to me on the sofa and searched until I found the cherry turnover I had chosen. "Well, I like him a lot better than I like *you*."

Smirking, he snatched a blueberry danish from the bag, then leaned back against the sofa to eat it.

I watched him, realizing it was the first time I had actually seen him eat. Maybe he wasn't so different from me and Braxton after all.

Sebastian noticed Ringo also watching him and a flash of fire shone in his eyes, making Ringo tremble.

Scratch that. He was still a devil. Even if we were sort of on the same side now, I couldn't let my guard down around him. He was using me, and I would use him too.

Of course, when it came to playing games with devils, they always came out on top.

3

MY WATCH BUZZED on my way to Emerald Heights. I lifted my wrist to see Dawn's number flashing at me. I had left a message for her the previous night, wondering if she could find out about Lucas, or the celestial woman who had been with him at the Circus.

"Well," Dawn said without greeting as soon as I accepted the call, "I haven't heard a single mutter about a full blooded celestial in the city, nor anything about the angelic, Lucas. But I *have* heard some other interesting tidbits."

I hopped over a crack in the sidewalk. "Go on." Greengate Park had come into view. There was a path through the park that led directly to the boundary of Emerald Heights.

"What will you give me in return?"

I shook my head, though she couldn't see it. "My half of the gossip, of course." Internally I thought, the

15

bare minimum of the gossip. Dawn was a colleague, and maybe sometimes a friend, but she would use any of the information against me if she could. Mostly to get me to return to work for her.

Dawn laughed, oblivious to my internal thoughts. "Word on the street is that there's a bounty on a celestial. Wouldn't happen to be the one you're looking for?"

I wanted to rub it in that Dawn was late on the gossip, but I also didn't want her thinking I knew too much about it. "I've heard whispers, but no. I think this woman might know my mom."

"You should really give that up, Eva."

"You should really mind your own business, Dawn."

"Me not minding my business is what makes me such a wellspring of information."

I rolled my eyes as I reached the green grass of the park. "My apologies. What else?"

"There's word a night runner named Eva Nix possesses important information on the bounty. And just this morning, the elves have claimed her as their own. Anyone who touches her will face retribution."

I stopped walking abruptly, catching odd glances from two humans with enough elf blood to give them pointed ears sitting on the nearby bench. "*What?*"

"Oh come on, Eva. You don't gain the protection of the elf king without knowing about it."

"Actually, you do." I kept walking, wondering what it meant. Though I supposed I would find out soon. I could already see the tall gates of Emerald Heights in the distance.

They were gold, glinting in the sun, with vines of ivy trailing up near the hinges. Maybe I should have visited Mistral first to ask for his advice, but after my encounter with Gabriel, I was hesitant. "I've got to go, Dawn. I'm about to walk into Emerald Heights."

Frantic chattering came from the other end of the line, but I hung up. I'd let her stew on that one for a while, thinking I had some tasty information for her. It might inspire her to learn more for me.

Warier than ever, I reached the gates and pulled one side slightly ajar. The metal was warm in my hand, moving smoothly and soundlessly aside. The open gate led to even more vibrant greens than what could be seen out in the park. I shifted to go over the boundary, then stepped onto the pale white cobblestone path, shutting the gate behind me. I started walking, observing the nearby homes. The buildings were quaint, white washed with brown trim. Most of my deliveries only came as far as the first few neighborhoods. Beyond them there were vast forests, and eventually a market square.

I had only been to the square on a few occasions, and it was where I would buy wolfsbane for Braxton if I had time. Anyone could grow it, but the elves had a certain touch with plants that made it more potent than anything else. The trees were also taller here, which was probably why all the buildings were made of wood.

Even the trees just outside the golden gates in the park were only half the size.

In one of those tall trees I noticed a raven watching me with beady black eyes. The bird was watching me way too intently for casual interest. Maybe it sensed I had recently come in contact with tasty pastries, but I doubted it.

I clutched the strap of my bag, wishing Ringo was inside. With the bag though, no one would bother me. Most of them would have seen me making deliveries at some point. No one would know that I was actually here to see their king, other than Elena and whoever she told.

And yet, my palms were sweating around my strap. Gabriel's warning repeated in my mind. Maybe the worry was unfounded. Maybe my magic wouldn't activate for anyone else, but it had already done so for three different people. Chances were, it would happen again.

I made my way beyond the first few neighborhoods into open forest, occasionally dotted with a distant white structure, smoke coming up from a narrow stone chimney. Unlike in the Bogs, the cobblestones beneath my feet were smooth and pristine. There were no puddles to step into, just vibrant green grass, wildflowers, and massive trees draped with vines. The trees provided ample shade as I walked, making me wish I had brought a coat. Eventually they closed in around the path, shrouding me in darkness.

Just when the darkness was beginning to feel eerie,

the sun came again as I reached an open meadow. Further down the cobblestone path I spotted a large creature with massive antlers.

I hesitated, wondering if I should hide, but I eventually decided to stand my ground. Elena knew I was coming. It wouldn't do to hide from one of her sentries—it would only prolong this whole experience.

And so I bravely kept walking until the creature came into clear view. It was a massive buck, and on its back rode Elena, her red hair shining in the sun.

She slipped down from the animal's back and jogged toward me. I was surprised that she wore just jeans and a yellow T-shirt. I had expected that in her own lands, the princess would be dressed like, well... a princess.

Elena reached me, her green eyes shining and her flushed cheeks making her freckles stand out. "You have no idea how glad I am to see you. It wasn't easy convincing my father to extend his protection. When I was alerted that a night runner was at the gates, I came straight away."

I wasn't sure who had alerted her, but I had passed by many homes. It stood to reason that someone had seen me. "Yeah, I heard about the protection thing. Not gonna lie, I was pretty surprised."

She gripped my arms. "You're important, Eva. I'm not going to have those vampires snatching you away, not even the Master of the City. I can take you the rest of the way to the palace." She nodded back toward the buck.

I stepped out of her grip, uncomfortable with her fervor. I looked skeptically at the buck. Riding a horse with Gabriel was one thing, the buck didn't even have a saddle.

Elena reached out and squeezed my arm again. "Don't worry, he's very gentle."

I winced at her repeated touch, worried that my magic might flare again, but nothing happened. No glow, no tingly feeling. I wasn't sure why I had expected it. I was pretty sure she had been born in this realm, but if she was a princess, she did probably have powerful magic. So maybe it was the other realm thing. But then, why Gabriel?

I shook my head at my own thoughts and Elena frowned.

"Oh, no, not you. Sorry, I've had a long morning. Let's go." On the back of a buck. To the elven palace. Yeah, completely normal.

Her smile resumed, if only a little more hesitant than before. "Do you want to talk about it?"

I shook my head. "Not really."

She gave me a smile that said she understood perfectly—though how could she?—then motioned me toward the animal.

I looked up at the beast. It was almost as big as Gabriel's horse. Its glassy eye rolled toward me, and I felt keenly aware that it was *judging* me. I glanced back at Elena. "You don't happen to have a step stool, do you?"

She hopped into motion. "Oh, forgive me, I'm just so used to being around other elves." She laced her fingers together, then lowered her hands to form a stirrup. "I'll just give you a boost."

I looked down at my dirty sneakers. "I'm not sure how I feel about stepping on a princess."

She scowled. "I'll have none of that. I get enough of that at home." She bent her knees and lowered her hands a bit more. "Now come on, you do owe me for getting my father to give you protection."

"You have an exceedingly strange way of calling in favors." I stepped into her hand, and she propelled me up onto the buck.

With my heart suddenly racing, I awkwardly tried to situate myself, not knowing what I should or shouldn't grab onto.

Elena hopped up nimbly behind me, then put her arm around my waist to steady me. Just as she did, the flutter of wings sounded overhead, then the raven I had seen near the gates touched down onto the buck's antlers. It looked over its shoulder at me with one black eye.

I looked back at Elena and whispered, "Did that bird tell you when I arrived?"

She gave me a bemused expression. "While I would love to telepathically speak with animals, that is not one of my gifts. I asked a friend near the gates to send word if she saw you."

Blushing, I turned forward.

Elena patted her heels against the buck's side and the creature turned around, then ambled back in the direction it had come. The raven stayed where it had landed, apparently content to come along for the ride.

"Are you ready?" Elena asked behind me.

"Ready for wha—"

She patted her heels again and the buck lurched forward, hooves clattering across the cobblestones. The raven shot up in a flurry of black wings. I clenched my thighs around the buck's broad back, hanging on for dear life. Elena maintained her grip on me, but her arm didn't feel quite as secure as Gabriel's. The meadow passed us by quickly, then more forest. Eventually we reached the market square, then continued onward.

"I've never been beyond the square!" I called back to Elena, wincing at the bruises forming on my ass.

She leaned in close to my ear. "It's mostly just uptight nobility further in. Nothing to write home about."

The cobblestone path in front of us widened, and the buck slowed as we reached what looked like a secondary town square. Colorful silk tents housed shops and seating areas where elegant elves sipped from teacups. The smell of fresh baked honey bread made my mouth water.

Elena leaned close again. "We can stop on the way

out if you want to buy anything. The quality is better here than at the main market."

Judging by the opulent clothing flowing from the elves milling about, I imagined that everything here was also three times as expensive. The tall elves walked with an air of dignity and importance—*nobility*.

Even though I had crossed boundaries hundreds of times, it was always a little jarring going deeper into the realms. Near the gates, things weren't quite so different from the city beyond. But deeper in, everything changed. Those who had actually come from other realms had done their best to create new homes to their liking.

I noticed some of the elves watching us as we made our way to the palace. They clearly recognized Elena, and were clearly not too sure about her human companion. I found myself wishing I had dressed up a little, even though Elena was just in a T-shirt and jeans herself.

The palace loomed up before us, high white walls incredibly different from the goblin's Citadel. Arched windows boasted glittering stained glass edged with gold. Flowering vines climbed up decorative pillars, the white stone beneath somehow not bearing a single mark of dirt or decay from the plants.

We went through a shaded alcove, then stopped near an outdoor stable. More deer, both bucks and doe, grazed on vibrant green grass.

Elena stopped our mount, then slid down to the

ground. Fortunately a tall male elf in a blue button up shirt approached and helped me down. I winced again at my bruises but stayed perfectly still, willing my legs to stop feeling like jelly.

The male elf led our buck away, and Elena gripped my arm, forcing me to hurry forward before I was ready. We ended up in another shaded alcove in front of a closed door.

Elena pulled me even closer, glancing around warily. When no one approached us, she heaved a sigh of relief, then lowered her voice. "So, I have something to tell you. My father doesn't know you're coming."

I pulled away from her, my jaw agape. "Then why am I here?

Her brow furrowed, she motioned me closer so she could continue to whisper. "You don't understand, Eva. He misses her."

"Who?" This was absolutely crazy.

She gave me an exasperated look. "The love of his life. My father has been heartbroken ever since he came to these lands."

"So he misses your mother?" As soon as I said it, I knew it wasn't right. Elena was young. The queen her father left behind wouldn't be her mother.

Her shoulders slumped. "No, I wasn't born through his first union. Once he was trapped here, he was forced to bond with another. But he and my mom," she shrugged, "they're more like just friends. She doesn't even live in the palace—she likes her cottage out in the woods. The one he really loves he had to leave behind." She grinned suddenly, her eyes sparkling. "I want to reunite them."

I wasn't sure whether to be pissed, or charmed by her motives. Maybe a little bit of both. "So why did he offer me his protection if he doesn't know about any of this?"

"I told him you're my friend," she said simply. "And today we're going to convince him that my friend needs the help of our court wizard to find her mother."

"So you want what everyone else does. You want to turn in my mother for the bounty."

Her eyes widened. "Oh, no, Eva. That's barbaric, and honestly, I don't believe the Realm Breaker actually exists. No, I brought you here to help you. To help us *both*."

My jaw fell open even wider, but Elena tugged me toward the closed door before I could argue. She opened it for us, then pulled me through into a hall with an impossibly tall ceiling. Massive arched windows with clear glass lined the hall, giving a sunny view of all of the greenery outside. Elena hurried us forward, our footsteps echoing against the walls around us.

My mind raced. If she didn't believe the Realm Breaker was real, then what could she want from me? Sebastian claimed he had seen it, that it wasn't just a myth, but apparently Elena didn't know that.

Eventually we made our way into a sitting room with more arched windows. Gentle rays of sunlight adorned shelves of books and other trinkets. In the center of the room a large table supported a game of chess, and around the board sat two older elves.

I didn't recognize either of them, but assumed one was the king judging by his blue robe embroidered with gold. His long hair was still the same perfect red as his daughter's, and only a few lines creased his face, though I knew he was centuries old. The other elf had hair so light blond it was almost white, and sharp features like a hawk. He gave me a shrewd once over, filling me with the urge to step behind Elena.

Then the elf king smiled, and the tension was broken. "I can see by your expression my daughter has taken you by surprise. She delights in keeping her *victims* off kilter."

She marched up to where he was seated and swatted his arm. "Hush, father. You'll scare her away."

He smiled. "Well we wouldn't want that, now would we?" He turned his attention back to me. "It's a pleasure to meet you, Eva Nix. I understand you've gotten yourself into a bit of trouble."

I winced. "Yeah, that's one way of putting it." His friend was still eyeing me, making me wonder if I should be bowing or curtsying or something. "I, um—"

"What she means to say," Elena smoothly interrupted, "is thank you for extending your protection."

He looked at his daughter adoringly. "As if I had any choice in the matter." He winked at me. "Not that I wasn't glad to help. I know dealing with vampires can be... difficult."

I gave Elena a meaningful look. Just what exactly had she told him?

"I must warn you though," he continued. "My protection can only extend so far. Elizabeta won't go against me, but some of her minions might. They are fools, the lot of them, if they actually think they will acquire a device that allows them to realm travel."

His friend flinched at the mention of realm travel, but the king didn't seem to notice.

"About that, father," Elena cut in again. "I was hoping you might grant Eva permission to meet with Crispin. She won't be safe until her mother is found, and I thought that Crispin might be able to aid her. He knows more about realm travel than any of the rest of us."

The other elf's expression soured further, and his cheeks were starting to turn red.

The king studied his daughter. "What exactly are you up to, Millelena?"

Elena glowered at the use of her full name. "I'm just trying to help my friend, father. What can it hurt?"

"Have you forgotten who we are discussing?" He softened his words with a small smile.

Elena lowered her chin, crossed her arms, and stared him down.

The king sighed, slumping in his seat. "Very well. I

believe Crispin is in his tower. If he is agreeable, you may seek his advice."

The blond elf's eyes looked like they were about to bulge out of his head as the king turned toward me. "But be warned, Eva. Crispin is a lovely lad, but you will do well to not get too caught up in his... *fervor*."

Elena hurried around her father and gripped my arm before I could ask what the hells he meant by *fervor*. "Thank you, father!" She tugged me away.

I caught one last look at the silent elf looking like his head was about to explode, while the king shook with quiet laughter, then Elena pulled us back into the hall and shut the door behind us.

"That was easier than I thought it would be," she beamed.

I crossed my arms. "Okay, but what did your father mean by *fervor*?"

She laughed. "Don't worry about it. Crispin makes some of the older elves uncomfortable, is all. But if anyone can help you, it's him." She took my hand then started tugging me back down the hall.

I realized in that moment, just as her father had realized, that resistance was entirely futile.

ELENA LED me through a maze of hallways I would never remember on my own until we reached a tower with a spiral staircase. As we went up, I peeked out the occasional window to the greenery beyond. Emerald Heights sure did live up to its name. It was stunning, all the growth bolstered by elven magic. I could hardly imagine what their homeland, a place where their magic actually flourished, might look like.

We reached the top of the tower and a heavy wooden door.

Elena gave me a reassuring smile, then turned to knock. "Crispin! It's me. My father agreed to everything!"

The door opened, revealing a tall male elf with tousled blond hair. The honey-colored locks were almost as shining as his pure blue eyes. Stubble lined his jaw, something you didn't see often amongst the elves. Most of them were fastidious when it came to appearances. He was dressed handsomely in a green shirt partially buttoned and rolled up at the elbows, and tweed pants.

He looked me up and down. "Well, she doesn't seem all too impressive."

Elena smacked his arm. "Move so we can come in."

He obeyed, observing me closely as I walked past him. There was far too much intelligence in those shining blue eyes, and I could already see why the king felt the need to warn me. It was in the way Crispin held himself, and the way his eyes danced with hidden thoughts. Here was a man who could convince you of almost anything.

He was so distracting I didn't feel comfortable

enough to closely observe the room, but I vaguely noticed a comfy seat by one of the windows, and next to it a small wooden table stacked high with books. The other side of the room boasted a massive table with papers, glass jars, and various thin metal devices I didn't recognize.

Crispin shut the door behind us, then stalked around me, once again looking me up and down. "She doesn't exactly shine with magic." He glanced at Elena. "From the way you've been talking, I was expecting a grand celestial spirit."

My cheeks heated. "Excuse me—"

"Trust me," Elena cut in, ignoring my discomfort. "She's special. She has vampires, angelics, devils, and who knows who else after her. If anyone can help you travel the realms, it's her."

She had forgotten to mention goblins, but I wasn't going to correct her. Maybe she didn't know everything after all.

Crispin finally concluded his observation and went to stand next to Elena with his arms crossed. "It's a good thing I trust you."

I glared at both of them.

"She's looking for her celestial mother," Elena continued, ignoring me. "But she can't fully shift."

Crispin raised a brow. "Then why do you think she can help us?"

"Because a devil thinks she can learn. And devils know everything, in the most infuriating way possible."

I couldn't argue with her there. But them not knowing that I could fully shift, at least for a moment, might prove problematic. If Crispin could help me figure things out to find my mom, he would need to know the truth.

Unfortunately, I already only trusted him as far as I could throw him. Which was not any distance at all.

Crispin stroked his chin, once again observing me. "As far as I know, half celestials can only travel to the near realms, but if a devil has interest in her, you may be onto something." He lowered his hand and grinned. "Either way, I'm not going to pass up an opportunity to study someone with celestial blood."

I narrowed my eyes at both of them. "Yeah, not so sure I want to be *studied.*"

Elena stepped toward me. "But you do want to maintain my father's protection, do you not? It would be difficult for you to continue your contract with the devil if you have to hide away behind a boundary."

My expression soured. So that was why she had gone the extra step of offering me her father's protection. I already owed her a favor, but that favor was just to come here. I considered saying no, but after what had happened to Braxton... I couldn't risk it again.

I gnawed my lip, looking back and forth between the two of them. My mind made up, I crossed my arms and looked at Elena. "I want your father's protection to extend to my roommate. If you can make that happen, Crispin can *study* me all he wants."

Elena gave me a wicked smile. "Deal."

I frowned. "Don't you need to talk to him first?"

She shrugged. "Don't worry about it. I can make it happen."

I looked doubtfully at Crispin. "And what do you hope to get out of this?"

"Knowledge." With one arm crossed, he waved the other hand in the air. "Power. All of the usual things, of course."

Oh gods, what had I just gotten myself into?

I sighed heavily. "I guess the only question left, is when do we start?"

Crispin's eyes sparkled. "I will need some time to prepare. Can you come here tomorrow?"

I looked at Elena again, wanting to make sure she could actually come through with what she promised.

She met my eyes, and gave me a nod.

My shoulders slumped. "I'll be here."

4

ELENA DROPPED me off at the golden gates with a fresh bag of wolfsbane for Braxton. Maybe I only picked it up because I felt guilty, but it would still make him happy, so why not?

For some reason I felt like it should be almost dark by the time I left Greengate Park behind, but in reality I had only been in Emerald Heights for a few hours.

I was about to step out onto the sidewalk when I heard the rustle of wings, then arms wrapped around me and I was suddenly airborne. I let out a scream and started to struggle, then we were so high up that I gripped the arms around me and went still, not wanting to be dropped. I could try to shift, but even if I managed to fully shift again, there was no saying if I would stick the landing, and the sidewalk was now way too far away.

My panicked thoughts cut off abruptly as I was

dropped onto the roof of a tall building, and Lucas landed beside me.

I scurried out of reach, pushing my windblown hair back out of my face. "What the hell, dude?"

He loomed over me, wings slightly spread to block out the lowering sun. A cool breeze picked up locks of his blond hair and ruffled the collar of his white linen shirt. "What were you doing in Emerald Heights?"

I gripped the strap of my bag, glancing around for the easiest way off the roof. There was a doorway leading down into the building, but it was probably locked, and I would have to get around Lucas to reach it. "I'm a night runner. I make deliveries." I stood up a little straighter, facing him. "Now where's my mother?"

He stalked toward me, his aggressive movements emphasizing his irritation. "I'm not allowed to kill you, but I still have to prevent you from finding her. This causes a significant issue for me."

I took a step back, but I was getting too close to the edge of the roof. He wasn't *supposed* to kill me, but that didn't mean he *wouldn't*. "Well sorry to be a pain in the ass, but get used to it."

He came too close and I flinched. I felt a pulse of magic from the card in my back pocket.

"You need to stop looking, Eva. You're not going to like what you find."

I gripped the strap of my bag hard enough to make my knuckles turn white, and forced myself to meet his angry eyes. "Well ever since you revealed my identity to everyone, I really don't have a choice."

He let out a bark of laughter, tossing back his head. "You believe I revealed your identity? Why would I make my life more difficult?"

I frowned. "Only you and Sebastian knew." I thought about Lilith, but Lilith didn't recognize me until after Ivan was already after me. Maybe someone else had noticed the resemblance, but who?

Lucas flexed his hands at his sides. "If you're not going to stop, I'm going to have to take you somewhere safe."

I stepped back again, then bumped into something solid. I glanced over my shoulder at Sebastian. "Took you long enough."

Sebastian tilted his head. "Did you not want to see what he had to say?"

I crossed my arms. "Fair point."

Lucas glared at both of us, then focused his attention on me. "You're a fool to trust a devil. Do you really want to get your mother killed?"

I fell silent, the question making me uncomfortable. Sebastian claimed he would be content with finding the offerer of the bounty, but I couldn't trust him entirely. If we found my mother first, would he turn her in?

"Just tell me where she is. Just put an end to this."

Lucas lowered his chin, but didn't respond.

"He doesn't know," Sebastian said behind me. "He is simply following orders."

Lucas wrinkled his nose and flashed his teeth, his angry eyes on Sebastian. "I hope you're not opposed to babysitting her constantly. I think you signed a longer contract than you realized."

Sebastian put a hand on my shoulder and pulled me back against him. I felt a flare of magic between us and tried to not show it on my face, but I could also sense Sebastian's surprise.

Not noticing, Lucas gave me a dark look. "I'll be watching you, Eva. You won't like what happens if you get too close."

He took off in a flash of white wings, leaving us in the cool breeze on our own.

I turned toward Sebastian, still feeling a pulse of magic between us, like a magnet drawing me closer. "It's getting worse," I whispered.

He nodded subtly, his attention mostly on our surroundings. "What happened with the elves?"

Could I really trust him? I would take his help, but if I could find my mother on my own...

"What do you think? Everyone wants the..." I glanced around, then whispered, "*object.*" There. That wasn't quite a lie. I didn't need to tell him that Elena wasn't actually after it.

"And can the elf king help you find it?"

I shook my head. "No. I don't think he has any answers." *But Crispin might,* I added internally.

Now I would just have to think of a good excuse to give Sebastian for going back there. "So what now?"

He didn't look at me, though he was still standing too close. "I'll take you home. There are some other avenues I need to explore. Keep the card on you, and don't go beyond any boundaries where I can't reach you."

I bristled at being ordered around.

He finally met my gaze. "Do as I say, Eva. I am your best chance at survival."

"Fine," I huffed. It was a good thing I only had a bargain of truth with Mistral.

He maintained eye contact for a moment longer, then his gaze drifted down to my lips.

I licked them reflexively, wondering if he was going to try to kiss me again.

Then a horn honked somewhere below us, and the moment was over.

He gripped my arm. "Let's go. You can tell me *exactly* what King Francis said to you on the way."

He tugged me toward the roof entrance, and I reluctantly followed. It would be dark by the time we reached my apartment, which meant traveling to the Bogs while Ivan and his vampires were awake. The elf king had offered me his protection, but it would probably be foolish to actually test it.

Not that I wouldn't do it, but I hated proving Gabriel right.

As soon as Sebastian was gone, I packed up a few things to head to the Bogs. With my bag slung over my shoulder, I reached into my back pocket for Sebastian's playing card. I looked down at the two of hearts, flicking the card with my finger. I was a little hesitant to leave it behind with Lucas still out there, but I would just have to make my journey quick. Once I was beyond the boundary, I would be fine.

As I set the card on my nightstand, I looked down at a folded piece of paper near my boots. Had that fallen from my pocket when I removed the card? It definitely hadn't been there this morning.

Ringo hopped down from his bookshelf to see what I was staring at.

Glancing at him perched on my bed, I picked up the paper and unfolded it. There were only a few words written, and I didn't recognize the handwriting. I might have tossed it out if the words weren't so terribly relevant to my current situation.

Do not trust the elves.

I stared down at the paper, wracking my brain to figure out where it had come from. The only people who had been close enough to slip it into my pocket were Lucas, Elena, and Sebastian. But I would have noticed, wouldn't I?

I stared at the paper for a moment longer, then folded it and walked over to stick it between two books on my shelf. It made me uneasy, but it hadn't really told me anything new. I couldn't fully trust *anyone*.

Leaving the paper behind, I grabbed a sweater, then opened the flap of my bag for Ringo. "Let's get out of here before Sebastian realizes we're gone."

He hopped into my bag without question. Braxton had headed out to visit his mom in the country, so I'd left his wolfsbane in his room. I was glad he had gone. He would be back in a day or two, but those were at least two days where I wouldn't have to worry about him. He would be with many members of his pack. No one would be taking him from there. Hopefully by the time he returned, the elf king's protection would be known throughout the city.

I headed out into the living room, then into the adjoining bathroom. It was already dark, so I was realistic enough to assume I might be staying the night in the Citadel. My toothbrush and deodorant went into the bag with Ringo. After they were both secure he held out his paw for one more thing, and I handed him the tube of toothpaste.

I thought once more about the strange note, then shook my head. Too many problems, and that was the least of my worries. My magic was reacting more strongly to Sebastian. I needed to speak with the goblin who had unlocked it all to begin with.

5

WE HAD JUST MADE it past the first goblin settlement when I spotted a tall figure on horseback further down the path.

I continued my approach until I was looking up at Gabriel. As much as I had been around him lately, I was still taken aback by the sheer size of him. "I'm beginning to think you just watch the gates all the time, waiting for me to arrive."

He frowned down at me. His cream colored linen shirt left his impressive arms bare, the even brown tone of his skin contrasting nicely with the lighter fabric. He had pulled his black hair away from his face, with only a few strands falling forward to frame his dark eyes.

"You know," I continued, "because you're always out here to find me?"

"Mistral can sense when someone crosses the boundary." He offered me his hand.

"That's not really much of an explanation." But I took his hand.

He lifted me onto his horse a little more gracefully than before, now that I was prepared for it. Once I was situated and his arm was around my waist, he turned the horse to ride back toward the Citadel.

I leaned into his warmth as he nudged the horse into a trot, my thin sweater not quite enough against the damp air of the Bogs.

"I'm glad you took my warning more seriously," his voice rumbled in my ear.

"Oh no, I'm not staying permanently. I just want to speak with Mistral about what happened."

His arm flexed around me. "He won't be able to entertain you until later this evening."

"Why not?"

He leaned closer to my ear as the horse picked up speed down a hill, pressing me tightly against his chest. "That is for him to say, if he so chooses."

I let it go. If I had to wait, then I would wait. I let Gabriel hold me tightly as the cool air pushed my hair back from my face. I wondered if goblins ran hotter than humans, because he radiated warmth. I also wondered if our skin would glow if I gripped onto his bare arm.

Eventually we neared the Citadel, but Gabriel veered off onto a different path.

I gripped his arm without thinking, then quickly released it. "Where are we going?"

"We have several hours to wait. I will show you around."

Excitement tickled up my spine. I was curious about the rest of the Citadel, but assumed I would never get to explore it. Not if I wanted to keep myself out of a cookpot. Our horse galloped down the narrow dirt road, past abandoned ruins and a few distant towers. Some of the towers were lit up, but too far for me to make out much else. A hint of woodsmoke hit my nostrils, making my stomach growl.

"Will there be food where we're going?"

He slowed the horse to a walk as I spotted lanterns in the distance. "You're a bottomless pit."

I was going to argue that I had skipped dinner to make it out to the Bogs more quickly, but then the village came into view over a rise and I shut my mouth.

It was different from the villages closer to the gates, where most of the homes were ramshackle and made of wood and other scraps. Here the homes were gray stone with lovely stained glass. Lights from within shone in a multitude of colors.

Gabriel guided our horse between the homes, stopping before a large tavern. The open double doors released the conversation and laughter emanating from within. The smell of baking bread and some sort of roasting meat made my mouth water.

Beyond the lights of the village I could see only trees and darkness. "Just how far do the Bogs go?"

Gabriel slipped down from the horse, then lifted the

reins over its head to tie to a wooden post. "Many of our people came over during the shift. Our lands reach far beyond the border of the city."

I looked around the glowing village, thinking of the elven palace. The shift had happened long before I was born, before the barriers existed. Celestials had shown peoples from other realms to this one. And in some cases, hundreds came across. But the magic of earth was different. They didn't have enough to get back. That was how the myth of the Realm Breaker came about. Those who were trapped claimed a celestial used a sword to cut away the old paths.

Some of the oldest creatures still hated celestials because of it, but we didn't see them often. They stayed deep within their own realms, which I was realizing were a lot larger than I could have imagined. And now... maybe they had been right. Maybe a celestial *had* trapped them all here.

Gabriel gripped my waist and lifted me down. I held onto his shoulders, meeting his eyes for a moment, but he quickly looked away. He released me to lead the way into the tavern.

I followed, hesitant at first, but I forgot about everything else as wonderful scents enveloped me.

Most of the goblins seated around the circular wooden tables looked more human like Gabriel, while a few others were more twisted with varying hues of skin and hair. Some of them eyed us curiously, but no one protested as we took an empty table and Gabriel gestured to the barkeep. The goblin came out from behind the bar, wiping a clean glass with a rag held in nimble purple fingers. His eyes were a darker shade of purple, and wary as he looked at Gabriel.

"Supper," Gabriel said, "and two pints of wild-flower mead."

Seeming relieved, the goblin bowed and scurried away, his rough-spun brown shirt flaring out behind him.

I was content to let Gabriel brood while we waited for our meals, because there was plenty for me to look at. Light fixtures made of cut glass hung from the ceiling, casting a glittering display across the dimly lit room. I wasn't sure if they burned oil, or if they were actually powered by electricity, which didn't seem possible this deep in the Bogs. I thought it more likely that they were powered by magic, or something else of goblin design.

Our food arrived. It looked like the goblin version of pot-roast with steamed potatoes and carrots, and a dark brown gravy. It smelled delicious, though I doubted it was as good as Gabriel's cooking.

I peered dubiously at the amber liquid in our glasses. If it was as strong as the alcohol I'd had with Mistral...

Gabriel smirked. "I thought something a little lighter might suit you better."

My shoulders slumped with relief, and I took the glass in hand. The mead had a strong floral scent, and the sweetness of honey. I took a sip and relaxed. Even if it was a little strong, I doubted Gabriel would leave me in a ditch.

He held his glass near his mouth, but didn't drink. "Tell me what happened with the elves."

I took another sip and lifted my brow. "What took you so long to ask?"

"I thought you might volunteer the information willingly."

Shaking my head, I lifted my fork and speared a small potato, then stuck it into my messenger bag. Ringo had been quiet, but the potato was quickly snatched from my fork. Chuckling, I speared another one for myself. "The meeting went well, though it wasn't quite what I expected. When I heard the king offered me his protection, I thought he wanted something from me."

Gabriel lowered his glass, his jaw agape. "King Francis offered you his protection?"

I nodded. "Yeah, but only because Elena asked him to. This was all her scheme to have me meet with their court wizard, Crispin."

His nose wrinkled at the mention of Crispin. "Though I know you do not heed any of my warnings, you would do well to exercise caution where Crispin is concerned. You cannot trust him."

I lifted my glass in acknowledgment. "Yeah, but you don't think I can trust anyone." I took a long swill. I hadn't realized just how tense I was until I finally started to relax.

He stabbed his fork into his meat. "What else?"

I shrugged. "Nothing. I'm going back tomorrow. He's going to help me figure out the finer mechanics of realm travel. He did it himself, you know."

"That is not a good idea."

I tilted my head and smiled. "Can you guess what I'm thinking now?"

He glowered. "That I don't think *anything* is a good idea?"

I laughed. "Finally, you're catching on."

I set my glass aside to cut into my meat. It definitely wasn't as good as anything Gabriel would make, but it warmed my empty stomach, which was good enough. I washed it down with more of the wildflower mead, and offered Ringo another potato.

Gabriel watched me eat, occasionally picking at his own food. Finally, he asked, "What does Sebastian think of you meeting with Crispin?"

I finished my drink and set the glass on the table, then shrugged. "I haven't decided how much I want to tell him about my time in Emerald Heights. But he's practical. I think if Crispin can help him get what he wants, then he'll be all for it."

"And what he wants is to turn your mother in for the bounty?"

"He doesn't care about that, at least that's what he says. He just wants the... object."

He set his glass aside and leaned forward, his dark eyes boring into mine. "The same *object* that Mistral wishes to acquire."

"That's the one," I said a little sarcastically.

Before I realized what was happening, the barkeep took our empty glasses and replaced them with two full ones.

"So you will give it to the devil?" Gabriel pressed.

I glanced at a few goblins looking our way, then leaned forward and lowered my voice. "Look, I don't know what's going to happen with the object, but if Crispin can help me learn to realm jump, maybe I can help Mistral *without* it."

His dark eyes scrutinized me, but he let it drop. He reached out for his filled glass and took a long swill.

Feeling a little uncomfortable with his scrutiny, I did the same.

Gabriel's expression softened as he watched me. "You're going to be drunk."

I shrugged. "It's been a while since I could let my guard down."

I could tell my words surprised him.

"But I'm safe with you, right?" I pressed. "You're so large, you could crush any enemies beneath your feet."

He glared at me, but as he lifted his glass to his lips, he muttered, "Yes, you're safe with me."

I barely felt the cold as we rode away from the village. I barely felt any of my troubles at all. Here, I was safe. At least for now.

I was tired enough to go to sleep, but at the same time the scent of rain and the horse's hooves pounding beneath us exhilarated me. As much as I wanted to discuss everything with Mistral, I didn't want the moment to end.

But still, I sat straighter as the horse finally slowed near the open gate, my eyes scanning the darkness for any sign of Mistral. I gasped as I spotted him. He looked like he'd been hit by a truck—metaphorically speaking.

Gabriel slipped from the saddle, then helped me down. I rushed toward Mistral huddling in the shadows of the wild shrubs, pushing away thoughts that maybe something had happened to him because of me. Because of the stupid game surrounding my mother.

I sensed Gabriel at my back as I reached the other goblin. "What's wrong? What happened?"

Mistral stood straighter, though it seemed to take great effort. "Nothing to concern yourself with. But I'm glad you came. We need to talk."

"But—"

Gabriel gripped my shoulder. "Inside."

I looked back at him, but his expression was unreadable. I felt a little shiver in my messenger bag, Ringo, uncomfortable with the tension.

Turning my gaze to Mistral, I nodded.

He led the way inside, and as we ascended the first set of stairs, I could see just how bone-achingly weary he was. I also noticed fresh mud on his boots and the hem of his trousers. More streaks of mud decorated his bare forearms where he had rolled up the sleeves of his midnight blue shirt.

I glanced back at Gabriel again as we reached the top of the stairs, but he only motioned me forward. We ended up in the sitting room where I had made my first bargain with Mistral.

As soon as Gabriel shut the door behind us, I turned to put both goblins in my sight. "Okay, what in the hells happened? Why are you two acting like someone died?" I narrowed my attention to Mistral. "And why do you look like you're about to keel over?"

Mistral walked toward the two chairs near the currently dormant fireplace, then slumped into one. He lifted his hand and snapped his fingers, and the flames flared to life. His hand fell limply into his lap, and he leaned heavily against the cushions.

Gabriel gestured for me to take the other seat.

I gave him an indignant look, making it clear that I didn't appreciate no one explaining things to me. But seeing how miserable Mistral appeared, I crossed the room and took the other seat.

He had closed his eyes, but opened them as I sat, the piercing gray orbs observing me closely. "Gabriel informed me about your magic reacting to Sebastian." He gave Gabriel a sidelong glance. "*And* to him."

I squirmed in my seat. I owed Mistral nothing, but it was still uncomfortable discussing making out with another man to one you had recently slept with. "Yeah, I'm not sure why it happens. Sebastian thinks it all started after you and I were together."

Mistral's brows lifted. "You told him?"

I shrugged. "He seemed to already know, and I had no reason to hide it."

One corner of his mouth curled into a soft smile, as if it pleased him that I wasn't trying to hide our tryst. "I'm afraid Sebastian may be right. I didn't realize it would happen. You must believe me."

"Well unless our bargain has somehow been dismissed, I have no reason not to."

He inclined his chin in acknowledgment.

"Gabriel told me you were changed because of it too," I pressed. "That you gained new magic. So why do you look so awful?"

He leaned his head back, angling his face toward the warmth of the fire. "It is nothing to concern yourself with. I will be well by morning."

"She visited the elves," Gabriel cut in, changing the subject. "*Crispin* wants to test her magic."

Mistral sat up straighter, his eyes suddenly alert. "What does *Crispin* have to do with anything?"

I sat up straighter too. "Why are you guys saying his name like that? What's the deal? He was a little intense, but he seemed nice enough."

"His *niceness* is not the issue," Mistral said tersely. "His blatant disregard for any and all consequences in his search for knowledge is the issue."

I frowned. "What does that mean?"

Mistral pinched his brow. It seemed I was giving him a headache. "That he pursues magical discovery, and he does not care who gets hurt in the process. Even when it's himself."

Ringo had finally popped his head out of my bag to listen to us.

When Mistral seemed too tired to explain further, Gabriel stepped forward. "Crispin was the last elf to come from his realm. Only fifty or so years ago."

I leaned forward in my seat. "He mentioned something about realm travel, but that's not possible. No one has come over that recently, other than celestials."

"He became trapped like all the rest of us," Mistral muttered. "But he still believes he can find a way to return."

I nodded along with his words. "Yeah, I got that, but that doesn't explain why you both are so worried about him."

Mistral met my eyes. "If he can use you for his own purposes, he will."

"Yeah, but so will you."

Neither of them seemed to have anything to say to that.

I looked at Mistral. "I'm not mad about it. I don't know what you awakened within me, but if I can use it to find my mother, I will."

Mistral lifted a brow. "And if Sebastian can awaken you further?"

I slumped back against my seat. I hadn't really thought that far ahead.

"There is a way to test it," Mistral continued, his eyes shifting to Gabriel.

I followed his gaze, but Gabriel was staring straight ahead. "You mean..." I trailed off, knowing exactly what he meant.

"A simple kiss will do," Mistral added. "If you react in the same way you did to Sebastian, we may be able to learn more about what's happening without his assistance."

I had a feeling he was right. There had been magic when I touched Gabriel's bare skin—not every time, but once was enough. "I can't just go around kissing people trying to get more magic."

Gabriel didn't react to my words, but he still wasn't meeting my eyes. Could I just stand up and kiss him? Hells, it wasn't like he wasn't attractive, though it was in a rugged and rather intimidating way.

I gripped the arms of my chair, part of me wanting to do it, but something held me in place. It just felt odd, to stand up and kiss someone with no preamble, especially in front of the other person I had been more than kissing.

When the silence had stretched on for too long, Gabriel lifted his chin. "I will prepare your bed chamber." He quickly turned away before anything could be said.

Once the door shut behind him, Mistral gave me a

knowing look. "We could easily learn just how far your magical reactions will go."

I glared at him. "I think you and I *both* know how far they will go."

"But we do not know if that is something simply between you and I, or if it can happen with others. You're a fool for not testing things out before your time with Crispin."

I turned my glare toward the fire and waved him off. "Well then I'm a fool. So what else is new?"

6

I LAID in bed next to Ringo, tossing a small decorative crystal from a shelf in the guest chamber into the air. I caught it, then tossed it up again, watching the splinters of overhead light shining through it.

"It's just that, you have to *want* to kiss someone, you know? It's too weird doing it just to test magic."

Ringo puffed up his fur around him, sinking further into his pillow. "You kissed Mistral to seal a bargain."

The crystal thunked into my palm. "He kissed *me*." Just the thought of the whole situation made me cranky. Mistral couldn't just go around kissing me, doing *more* with me, then pushing me to kiss other people.

I gripped the crystal and sat up in bed. "I'm going to find Mistral."

Ringo buried his face into the pillow, not giving me a reply.

I stood with a huff, leaving the crystal on the bed as

I went for the door. I went out into the hall, looking both ways, but I didn't see anyone. Not even any tiny goblins loitering on the stone ledges of the walls.

I strode toward Mistral's chamber, preparing to knock, but on second thought I simply threw the door open... and was met with an empty room.

I heard footsteps and turned to see Gabriel heading my way.

I put my hands on my hips. "Where is he?"

He stopped several paces back, giving me my space. "Resting. He must not be disturbed."

My anger flared, and I took a step toward him. "What's going on? You guys know *everything* about me. This isn't fair."

He narrowed his dark eyes at me as he closed the space between us. "Your quarrel is not with me. And it is not for me to share someone else's situation."

I had to crane my neck awkwardly to look up at him. Once upon a time him looming over me with that dark look would have made me flinch away, but not now. "But you both would rather guard your secrets than help me with Crispin tomorrow."

He leaned down toward my face. "We are *trying* to help you Eva. But you would rather run in blind than lower yourself to kiss me."

My jaw fell open and my breath whooshed out of me like I had been punched. He had obviously gotten the wrong idea. "It's not about not *wanting* to kiss you."

"It is not an issue," he muttered. "You will do as you choose. But do not say we are not trying to help you."

"And I wouldn't be *lowering* myself to kiss you," I continued. "I would obviously be raising myself, because you're so gods damned tall."

His eyebrow twitched at my ridiculous attempt to lighten the situation. I was still pissed, but now felt a little bad because I was pretty sure I had hurt his feelings.

"And what if it works?" I pressed. "What if we kiss and awaken new magic in both of us? Are you going to expect more from me?"

He lowered his chin. "I would never do that."

I realized I had once again offended him. "You can't blame me for thinking it with the position I'm currently in."

He took a step back and let out a heavy sigh. "I suppose not. Now, I will escort you back to your room. You will not see Mistral until morning. Please do not ask me about it again." He turned and started walking back toward my room.

I hurried after him. "Just like that, you'll let the issue of the kiss drop?"

"It is not an issue. If you do not wish to do it, that is your choice." He reached my door, turning to open it.

Wanting to see his face as he spoke, I stopped him with a hand on his arm. Where our bare skin touched, a slight glow emanated.

Gabriel stiffened, looking down at his arm, then at me.

With my heart suddenly thundering, I used my grip on his arm to balance as I stood on tiptoe. The moment our lips met, power flared between us.

I expected a chaste kiss, nothing more, but then he lowered his hands to cradle my face, pulling me closer. His tongue dove into my mouth, and I twined my arms around his neck, lifting myself to better accommodate his height. His large hands moved to my waist, making me feel tiny with the way they engulfed me.

The magic increased, pounding against my skull as arousal tightened my body. It wasn't the same as with Sebastian—there was no thrill of darkness to it—but there was another sort of thrill, like the deep, resonant heartbeat of the earth, echoing in my bones.

His hands moved lower, cupping my butt to lift me before he turned us so my back was pressed against the wall. He drank me down, like a steady tower against the crashing waves of wild magic.

There was so much inside of me. So much that I never realized was there.

He broke the kiss, looking down at me with heat and maybe a touch of confusion. "Eva," he whispered.

Struggling to catch my breath, I slid down until my feet hit the floor.

He stepped back so I wouldn't be completely squashed against the wall. "Eva, I—"

I gripped the knob of my door and slipped inside, shutting it behind me, then leaned against the wall. My entire body felt like it was burning, and not in a bad way—

But the magic. It made it too hard to think. I could have just as easily ripped his clothes off right there in the hall. With my back against the wall, I sank to the floor.

Ringo hopped down from the bed and scurried over to me, his large eyes wide with concern.

I buried my face in my palms and shook my head, trying to calm my racing heart. "I don't know what's happening to me, Ringo."

I felt his soft little paw on my wrist, the light touch releasing my tears.

I wasn't even sure why I was crying, but it probably had something to do with my entire life being turned upside down.

And maybe something to do with the fact that in all likelihood, things would only get worse.

)) ● ● ● ● ● ((

I wandered out into the hall with Ringo the next morning, surprised no one had woken us. I had grown oddly accustomed to waking up with Gabriel standing over me, for one reason or another. But today, nothing.

Finding Mistral's chambers still vacant, I wandered further down the hall until I found the goblin himself.

He held a plate in each hand, and I smelled maple syrup.

He reached me and handed me a plate. "I thought you might prefer to eat in your room, unless you're no longer upset?"

I took the plate, looking down at a fluffy stack of pancakes. I never would have taken Mistral for a pancake person, but he had an identical plate in his other hand. It made me smile.

"It's fine. It was just a long day yesterday. Where is Gabriel?"

Mistral studied my face as he answered, "His horse is gone. He is somewhere out in the Bogs."

I sucked my teeth. Had he run away because of me? As the night wore on, I had regretted cutting him off so abruptly. But everything had just been so overwhelming.

I moved my plate away from my messenger bag as a little blue paw tried to snatch one of my pancakes. "Should we eat outside? I could use some fresh air."

We were near the study, and Mistral gestured toward the open door and the balcony beyond.

We ended up seated on the low stone wall with a rather perilous fall below us. If I lost my balance, would I be able to shift in time to save myself, just like I had shifted to save Braxton?

I wasn't betting on it. At least not until I'd had a chance to explore things further. I lowered one leg enough that I had a foot on steady ground, my knee coming close to brushing Mistral's.

Mistral was silent as I took a bite of my pancakes, closing my eyes as a cool breeze tickled my face. I took a deep breath of rain-scented air, then gazed out across the forested land. "I didn't realize how much land you have here until Gabriel told me last night."

Mistral followed my gaze. "It has been my home for a long time, and I am grateful for it."

The silence stretched on between us as I ate my pancakes. He seemed better than he had the previous night, but there was still an edge of exhaustion dragging at his features.

"I think I'll be okay today with Crispin. I don't think I'll react to him, and maybe he can help me learn something. I know you guys don't trust him, but he *did* manage to realm travel relatively recently. If anyone can help me figure it out, it's probably him."

Mistral finally looked at me, his gaze sharper than before. "Why do you believe your magic won't react to him?"

I turned my attention back to the distant greenery, combing over the thoughts that had plagued me all night. "I think—" I hesitated, trying to come up with the best way to put it into words. "I think I have to feel something for the other person involved. To have the... reaction."

"And you feel something for Sebastian?"

I glared at him. "It doesn't have to be a *positive*

emotion. He irks me, but he has also saved my life several times. It's complicated."

Mistral nodded, accepting my vague explanation. "Just be careful. He'll use you if he can."

"Obviously." I fought the urge to touch his long white hair as a soft tendril lifted in the cool morning breeze. I knew I should still be irritated with him, but it was difficult with the nice morning, pancakes, and him being so pleasant. "You didn't seem bothered by the idea of me kissing Gabriel."

He tilted his head. "Should I be?"

"Most men would be."

He was silent for a time, his untouched plate of pancakes balanced on one knee. I was about to break the silence when he finally spoke. "You know, it's not just for power, nor for the possibility of realm travel."

"What's not?"

He met my eyes solidly. "My interest in you. It's not just about that."

"What is it about then?"

One corner of his mouth curled up. "Are we fishing for compliments?"

I smiled. "Absolutely."

He laughed, setting his pancakes aside. "I will admit, initially I was simply intrigued by a woman of celestial blood who would so easily agree to a bargain. Especially a woman who already had a contract with a devil. I thought you were either stupid, or you knew something that the rest of us didn't."

I narrowed my eyes. "And what do you think now?"

"Impulsive, perhaps. But not stupid. And kind. I tricked you into multiple bargains, and you showed me kindness and compassion."

I lifted my brows, caught off guard by his honesty. "You do realize you showed me the same, right?"

"Perhaps you bring it out in me."

I set the rest of my pancakes by our feet where Ringo was huddled in my bag. It didn't take him long to reach his blue paws out for the fluffy gooey mess. I was going to have to throw my bag into a washing machine later.

With my hands free, I scooted a little closer to Mistral. "So you're saying you like me."

He laughed. "Yes, Eva. I'm saying I like you."

"Because I kind of got mixed signals when you told me to kiss your closest friend."

He smirked. "And that is precisely why I asked you to kiss him. He is my closest friend. I trust him with my life, and yours." He leaned close and lowered his voice. "And I'd much rather have you kissing him than a devil."

I watched his face for any hint of discomfort, but it wasn't like he could lie to me. He meant every word he said. "So you'd be totally okay with it?" I thought back to my moment with Gabriel the previous night. I wasn't sure if Gabriel had told Mistral, or if he would.

"As long as you don't entirely choose him over me," a half smile softened his words, "I would be quite interested to see how Gabriel might affect your magic."

He smoothed a finger up my wrist, making the magic flare between us. My whole body went tight, suddenly aching to be touched. My voice was breathy as I asked, "And what do you think would happen if you and I were together again?"

"There's only one way to find out." He leaned closer, maintaining his hold on my wrist.

I wanted nothing more than to find out right then and there, but, "I have to meet Crispin this morning."

He used his other hand to push my hair aside, then grazed my neck with his lips. Goosebumps prickled across my bare arms. "Return to us afterward," he whispered in my ear.

A lump formed in my throat. *Us*, not *him*. I wasn't sure if I was ready for anything else, but I nodded. I wouldn't mind a repeat of my time with Mistral, and after what he had just admitted...

Maybe it could be *more*. Maybe it was more. But I would be foolish to think that way. I couldn't let myself develop feelings for a guy who wanted nothing more than to go home to another realm.

Especially when I planned on being the one to help him do it.

7

I HAD HOPED to see Gabriel during our ride to the gates. I wasn't sure what I would say to him if I did, but I hated how I had left things the night before. Unfortunately, we saw no sign of him, and even more unfortunately, Sebastian was waiting outside the gates when we arrived.

It was a mostly sunny day, but a single thick cloud cast him in a pool of shade. His crisp white shirt contrasted with a fitted gray suit vest and slacks. He looked bored as we dismounted on the other side of the gates, but I knew it was an act. He probably went to the location of his calling card—my apartment—before moving on to the next place he thought I might be. He wasn't bored. He was pissed.

Mistral stayed by my side as I moved to open the gate.

With his attention on me, Sebastian lifted his hand,

my playing card between two of his straightened fingers. "If you don't keep this with you, I won't be able to help you when there's trouble."

"She is safe here," Mistral replied before I could say anything.

Sebastian's eyes drifted to Mistral. "She could come to harm right where I'm standing and you wouldn't be able to do anything."

Mistral glared at Sebastian. "She could come to harm right where you're standing, and you wouldn't do anything unless she offered you something in return."

Sebastian's brow lifted. "Have you truly convinced her that you care? That you want more from her than the bounty on her mother's head?"

I abruptly pushed open the gate, glaring at Sebastian. "That's pretty rich considering *your* motives."

"I only speak the truth to Eva," Mistral said. "The same will never be said of you."

Sebastian opened his mouth and I held up a hand to cut him off. "I need to get to Emerald Heights, and I want to change first, so whatever is going on between the two of you will have to wait."

His eyes widened briefly, and I realized I had messed up. "You intend to return?"

I had forgotten that I'd only told Mistral and Gabriel about that. "Yes. The court wizard knows a bit about realm travel. I want to ask him some questions."

Sebastian lowered his chin, his expression clearly stating that he knew I wasn't telling him everything.

"Then I will escort you home to change your clothing, since no one *else* is offering." His eyes were on Mistral as he said it.

Mistral took my hand before I could step over the boundary, then placed a light kiss on my knuckles, keeping his eyes lifted to my face. Magic tickled my fingers. "I hope you will remember what we spoke about."

Since that could mean far too many things, and none of them would I want to discuss in front of Sebastian, I simply nodded. "I'll come back when I can."

He released my hand, and I stepped over the boundary.

Sebastian touched the small of my back to turn me away from Mistral, and I had a feeling it was only for the other man's benefit.

I glanced back as we started walking, meeting Mistral's gaze for a moment before we went around a bend in the path. The gate was closed at my final glance, though I hadn't heard it move.

Once we reached the first street, Sebastian lifted his hand at the oncoming traffic and a cab immediately stopped for us. I gave him a suspicious look, but when he opened the door for me, I got inside. During certain times of the day it could be impossible to hail a cab in the city. I wasn't going to gripe if he had used magic to help us out. I had places to be, after all.

We sat in the silence of the air-conditioned cab, with me squirming in my seat, breathing shallowly around the smell of stale cigarettes. I still couldn't quite tell what Sebastian's mood was, though verbally sparring with Mistral had seemed to bring him some enjoyment.

Once the cab let us out near my neighborhood and we were away from the potentially prying ears of our driver, I turned to face Sebastian. I really didn't want him to ask me questions about Crispin, so I beat him to the interrogation punch. "What was with all your comments to Mistral? I know you guys have history, but no one seems to want to talk about it."

His smile was pure ice. "You share too much with him. You seem to think he can protect you, and I felt it my prerogative to let you know that it's not the case. Mistral cannot leave the Bogs."

My jaw fell open. I had suspected it, but part of me couldn't believe it was true.

Sebastian grabbed my arm and pulled me out of the way as a cyclist whizzed past us. "And you *do* seem to need the protection."

My heartbeat picked up as he continued gripping my arm. "How do you know he can't leave the Bogs?" Not that it didn't make sense. Now I knew why he had sent Gabriel to my apartment rather than coming himself.

Sebastian surprised me by actually answering, "Because that was the bargain he struck with me. His mother maintained the magic of the Bogs before him. When she died, he begged me to help him take her place—to create a contract of sorts between himself and the land. Being unable to leave the Bogs was the price he paid."

"But how does that benefit you?"

He tilted his head. "Not everything has to benefit me, dear Eva." He released my arm and gestured for me to start walking.

Reluctantly, I did, though I kept him in my sights. "You're a real piece of work, you know that?"

"You're too kind." We reached my favorite café, and he stopped outside the door. "I thought we might like to pick up some of those delightful pastries on the way home."

I looked up at him suspiciously. "Is that why you had the cab drop us so far from my apartment?"

Instead of answering, he opened the door for me.

He was being far too pleasant after I had disobeyed him and left the card behind. I hesitated in the doorway. "You're not going to try to kiss me again, are you?"

Still holding the door open, he leaned close to my face. "Oh, dear Eva. The next time we kiss, it will be because you *begged* for it."

"Yeah, not likely." His laughter followed me into the café.

At least I was getting pastries. And at least he couldn't follow me into Emerald Heights. Together, he and Crispin would be utterly intolerable.

Despite my protests, Sebastian escorted me all the way to the border of Emerald Heights. It was almost like he didn't trust me. Almost like it had bothered him that I had run off to the Bogs the first chance I got, telling Mistral all my secrets while spilling none of them to *him*.

Elena waited just beyond the golden gates, wearing a loose green flannel and jeans. She wrung her hands in a rare display of nerves. Two massive bucks waited further up the cobblestone path.

"Thank goddess you're on time." She hurried to open the gates, not even acknowledging Sebastian's presence. Her red hair hung across her face for a moment, and when she pushed it back, I could see the panic she was trying to rein in.

I took one side of the gate from her, pulling it open the rest of the way. "What happened?"

She finally glanced at Sebastian, then back at me. She gnawed her lip. "If I knew what was good for me, I wouldn't tell anyone about this, but I think you may be the only people who can help."

I lifted a brow. "People?"

She glanced around her, then moved closer to us, stepping across the boundary. She lowered her voice. "Crispin was doing an experiment to prepare for today, and something happened."

I narrowed my eyes. "What kind of something?"

"Shh." Her eyes shifted. "You'll just have to come and see. Both of you." She gave me a meaningful look.

Did she mean Sebastian? "Um, you know he can't come across the boundary, right?"

She reached into her jeans pocket, then produced a small green glass leaf. "His temporary invitation," she explained. "My father is aware of what has happened."

I looked over my shoulder at Sebastian. "Are you following any of this?"

"For once, I'm just as flummoxed as you." He leaned in to observe the leaf, flicking his eyes toward me. "But don't get used to it."

Elena shifted her feet impatiently. "Will you do this for Eva's sake?" She held the leaf toward Sebastian.

He tilted his head, eyeing the leaf. "I will witness what you wish us to see, but I promise nothing else."

I was honestly surprised he wasn't asking for more. But then again, he was actually getting an invitation into Emerald Heights. There was no saying what kind of trouble a devil could stir up amongst the elves. Or maybe he just wanted to catch me in a lie...

But Elena didn't seem to consider any of that. Nodding to herself, she stepped back across the boundary, then extended her hand with the leaf in her palm. "Place your hand over mine."

Sebastian obeyed, his long fingers covering the base of her wrist. Green light flashed between their palms, and when he lifted his hand, the leaf was gone. Elena moved back, and he stepped effortlessly across the boundary.

I shook my head. "Just when I thought I had seen

everything." I shifted slightly, stepping across the boundary to join them.

Elena eyed Sebastian warily, like she hadn't been the one to just invite him into her realm. I wondered what her people might think of their princess letting a devil in. She had to be absolutely desperate to do so. Just what had happened to Crispin?

I opened my mouth to ask just that, but Elena was already walking toward the waiting bucks.

"Two bucks for three riders?" I asked as I followed after her.

She glanced back as she reached the massive beasts. "You didn't seem very comfortable with riding. I thought you might be safer with me."

My shoulders relaxed. I didn't want to ride with Sebastian for a *myriad* of reasons, but primarily because I didn't know if my magic might kick up again. "Well he kind of does this black whooshy thing. I'm sure he can just meet us there now that he's across the boundary." I jumped when I realized he was standing directly behind me, close enough to touch.

"I will ride," he said simply.

I gave him a sidelong glance, but he didn't return the attention, and Elena was already waiting with her fingers laced to boost me onto the buck.

"My, aren't we all being terribly agreeable?" I muttered, stepping away from Sebastian.

Elena launched me onto the buck, and I made an effort to settle in comfortably after her comment about my riding. With the grace of a gymnast, she hopped up behind me, scooting in close and putting her arm around me.

I looked toward Sebastian, hoping he would have trouble climbing atop the other buck, but he simply guided the beast to a tree stump, using it to boost himself. He ended up on the buck's back with not a single hair out of place.

Infuriating.

As we started riding, Elena looked over at Sebastian. "Your invitation into our realm will wear off around nightfall, just so you're aware."

"I suspected as much." He observed the greenery around us, and the distant homes.

"Good." Elena's arm tightened around me as she patted her heels against the buck's sides, and the beast lurched forward.

I gritted my teeth and held on for dear life, glaring at Sebastian every so often as he rode effortlessly beside us.

8

WE DIDN'T SEE the king or his grouchy friend on our way to Crispin's tower. No one in the square had questioned Sebastian's presence, and soon the three of us stood outside the door I had gone through the day before.

Elena stepped close to me before opening it. "What you're about to see stays between us. Agreed?"

Sebastian lifted a brow, but nodded.

I had never seen him so accommodating, but I also knew him well enough by now to guess that his curiosity was keeping him civil. Not only was he being allowed within elven lands, perhaps for the first time ever, but he was also about to meet someone who had realm traveled relatively recently.

Elena opened the door, then gestured for us both to walk in ahead of her.

I stepped into the room first, glancing around for just

a moment before my jaw fell open. Crispin stood near one of his many bookshelves—well, he kind of stood near it. I could see him, but he was looking a little... see-through.

Sebastian waited beside me while Elena shut the door behind us, then he approached Crispin, who was looking utterly miserable. It was clear that he could see us, but he didn't speak. For all intents and purposes, he seemed like a ghost. His mouth moved, but we couldn't hear the words coming out.

Sebastian crossed his arms, bracing one hand beneath his chin. "What was he trying to do?"

Elena gave me a wary glance before answering, "I think he was trying to realm jump. Or at least maybe open up a pathway? I don't really understand any of it, and he's not exactly able to tell me anything. He can't touch a pen to write out what happened."

Sebastian looked back at me.

I held my hands up, palms out. "Hey, my knowledge on all this is way less than either of you. Why do you think I'm here?"

He watched me for a moment longer, then lowered his eyes to the floor beside him, making it clear he wished me to approach.

Reluctantly, I moved to his side, wary of stepping too close to Crispin. The elf's blue eyes were now filled with hope—*entirely* unfounded hope. He mouthed something at me. *Portal*, maybe.

"Is he saying he made a portal?"

"I think so," Elena said behind us. "I managed to read his lips a bit. *Portal*, and *Eva*, I think. The devil was my idea. I had hoped he would be with you, or that you could at least summon him."

I turned to find Sebastian watching me.

"What do you think?" he asked.

Frowning, I looked at Crispin, daring to reach a hand out toward him. When nothing bad happened, I stepped closer and tried to touch his chest, but my hand went right through him.

He winced, and I quickly withdrew my hand. "I think he's stuck between realms. Wherever he was trying to go, he didn't fully make it. It's kind of like what I can do to step over boundaries, but he went a little further. Shifting isn't exclusive to celestials. We're just better at it." I looked at Sebastian, thinking of how he could simply disappear in a flash of darkness. But he couldn't reach the far realms, else he'd have no interest in me. He could probably still travel to the hells, the closest parallel realms to earth, and that was it. "In some ways," I added for his benefit.

"How do we bring him back?" Elena asked.

I stepped back by Sebastian. "Oh, I have no idea. I've never gotten stuck before. If he can't find the pathway back, it would take someone else who can actually travel between realms to reach him." I glanced at the various vials and instruments scattered across Crispin's worktable, then at the elf in question. "It would help to know how he traveled in the first place, I think."

Miserable, Crispin pointed at an open journal at one end of the table.

"It's gibberish," Elena explained.

I walked a wide path around Crispin to observe the journal. I skimmed a few lines, seeing just what Elena was talking about. It was all symbols and charts I didn't recognize. Realizing Sebastian was reading over my shoulder, I looked back at him.

"Alchemy," he said. "Unfortunately, not one of my many considerable talents."

I side-stepped away from Sebastian, careful not to touch him as I turned back toward Elena. "Aren't there any other elves here who can read it? I imagine Crispin isn't the *only* one."

Elena's cheeks reddened and she wasn't quite meeting my eyes.

Sebastian chuckled. "Her father has ordered her not to tell anyone. I imagine experiments regarding realm travel are forbidden?"

I looked back and forth between him and Elena. "What? Why?"

Elena's shoulders slumped. "Yes, besides the three of us, only my father knows what has happened. I had to tell him so he would allow Sebastian in, but no one else must know."

Thoroughly confused, I waited for further explanation, but Elena simply hung her head.

"But why?" I pressed. "What's the big issue?"

Sebastian stepped close to my side again. "Realm travel is obviously a touchy subject with the elves. On one hand, they do not want to give their people false hope. On the other, they do not want to anger them for repeating the mistakes of the past." He leaned in even closer, close enough that his dark magic slithered up my skin. "They fear ending up somewhere far, far worse."

I furrowed my brow, still not entirely understanding the secrecy. "But don't you think it would be worth letting in a few more people if they can help him?" I asked Elena.

"Perhaps," she sighed. "But I believe the two of you are his best chance, and so does my father. So why not ask you first?"

"You *did* save Braxton the other night," Sebastian said vaguely.

I whipped my eyes toward him. He was hinting at me fully shifting, which maybe I could do if I understood where Crispin had actually gone, but I had no idea. And I didn't know how he had gotten there.

Sebastian stepped toward Elena before I could say anything else. "You will need to sign a contract. Nothing that happens in this room reaches any other ears or eyes." He lowered his voice. "For dear Eva's safety, of course."

"*For my safety*, my ass." I stormed up behind him. "And if it's my ass getting risked, you don't get any new contracts out of it."

He looked over his shoulder at me with one brow lifted. "Oh? So you would like the information you are about to reveal in helping this poor pathetic elf to be available for any pointed ears that will listen?"

I crossed my arms. "I don't even know if I can do anything."

"But you will try. Or am I mistaken?"

I glowered. "Yeah, I'll try."

He humored me with a pleasant smile. "Then allow me to ensure your secrets are kept. Unless you have the power to create entirely binding contracts yourself?"

I huffed. "Okay, fine. But the contract is just to keep that *one* secret. Nothing else."

"Of course."

Elena was looking back and forth between the two of us. "What am I missing?"

"Eva may be able to help you," Sebastian explained. "But you will need to sign a contract. What you will see may prove dangerous for her should the wrong people learn of it."

Elena looked at me. "Is he trying to trick me?"

I shrugged. "Probably. But whatever is in the contract, he has to follow as much as you do."

She straightened, lifting her nose in the air and tossing her red hair behind her shoulders. "Very well. Whatever happens in this room today, we will speak of it to no one. *All* of us."

"And you may not tell your father," Sebastian added.

Elena's eyes flared. "He's going to give me hell, but fine. But this only applies to anything learned here today. Crispin and Eva's work in the future is fair game."

Sebastian extended his hand and Elena took it, sealing the contract.

I glanced at Crispin, who still looked miserable as he watched the entire scene. It didn't seem he had much faith in us, and he was probably right to feel that way.

Sebastian released Elena's hand and turned to me with a wicked smile. "Now, dear Eva, do fetch this poor elf so we can get on with our day."

)) ● ● ● ● ● ((

I stood facing Crispin with my palms extended toward him. He mirrored me with a look of cautious optimism in his eyes.

Sebastian stood far too close to my back, whispering in my ear. "What happened with Braxton, Eva?"

I shook my head. I knew he was trying to help, but I had no idea how I'd shifted to save Braxton. "I don't know. I was desperate to save him."

Sebastian's warm breath caressed my earlobe, summoning forth a trickle of magic. "Then feel desperate now." He was like a dark force behind me. A literal devil on my shoulder whispering in my ear.

I looked at Crispin, trying to summon the same desperation to save him, but I didn't even know him.

And it didn't help having Elena leaning against the nearest windowsill, silently watching us.

Sebastian lightly gripped my arms from behind, just the thin fabric of my shirt between our skin. "There are many realms that are simply pockets of space. If it helps, one such realm is likely where the elf is trapped. If he cannot escape, he's going to starve to death. Or at the very least, go mad in his solitude."

I stiffened in his grip. I wouldn't wish that on anyone, but, "I still can't feel anything. I sense the part of him that is here, but nothing else. I don't know how to find a path."

"Then think of your time with the goblin prince," he whispered.

I inhaled sharply, caught off guard by his words. "You know," I said through gritted teeth, "you're really not helping." I glanced toward Elena, but she showed no sign of hearing his words.

Sebastian stepped closer so that my back grazed his chest. He lowered his cheek against mine, making my breath hitch. "Would you rather think of me instead?"

My cheeks burned. "In your dreams, asshole."

"In my dreams, or in *yours*?"

My neck heated along with my cheeks because he was right on the money with that one. "You're not helping."

"And you're not getting anything done. I can feel your fear. You're running scared, like usual."

Anger flared through me, and along with it a spark of magic. "Listen you son of a—"

I started to turn, but he gripped my arms hard enough to bruise. "Focus on the elf, Eva."

I glared at Crispin, even though my glare was meant for Sebastian. "You don't understand. You were probably raised in the hells with lots of other little devils. You probably wielded your magic before you could even talk."

"Poor Eva," he taunted. "So pathetic. So alone. I learned my magic because I *wanted* it. You're just too scared to try."

I wanted nothing more than to turn around and slap him, but I kept my attention on Crispin. I could feel my magic just below the surface, summoned by my anger. Not just anger at Sebastian's harsh words, but anger that despite them, it felt good to have him pressed against my back. Far too good.

Crispin's eyes had gone a little wide at our exchange, though I didn't think he could actually hear us. Maybe he was a better lip reader than Elena.

"I'm not scared," I muttered under my breath. But I was humiliated.

Wanting nothing more than to just end the situation, I pulled away from Sebastian, reaching for my magic in the only way I knew how—to shift across a barrier. With heat and anger and magic pulsing through me, I shifted as much as I could, then walked right into Crispin.

"Don't!"

But Crispin's words came too late, mostly because I could only hear them once I crossed whatever boundary stood between us.

We were in a small stone room. I could distantly hear the ocean, but there were no doors and no windows. The only light came from the crumbling ceiling far overhead.

Panicked, I looked around for Sebastian and Elena, but I couldn't see them at all. I had shifted fully.

I looked at the dejected elf in front of me as he hung his head, shaking it back and forth.

I had shifted fully.

And now I was trapped.

9

"Not exactly what I had in mind," Crispin said to my back.

I pushed against the nearest stone wall. It couldn't be real. I couldn't be entirely trapped here, and without anything to focus on to bring me back. Worse, whatever I had done had pushed Crispin all the way through too.

"You still can't see them?" My voice was tight with panic.

"As I already explained, you coming here seems to have fully opened the pathway I was trying to create. You brought me all the way here, away from the tools I need in order to return." I looked back at him as he crossed his arms and tilted his head. "Not that my situation is really worse, other than my only hope of escape being trapped here too."

I turned fully toward him. "What were you even trying to do? Why come here?"

His blue eyes were the dullest I had yet seen them as he answered, "I was only trying to chart the path. I thought if you could see a path, it might help you to travel." He shrugged a shoulder. "I suppose in a way, I was correct." He gestured toward me. "You're here. You realm jumped. Although, this little pocket is very close to earth. I would not yet task you with traveling to the elven realm. You would probably end up trapped inside a star."

Clouds shifted across the crumbling hole overhead, darkening the small space. When night fell—*if* night fell in this place—we would be left in total darkness. "What do you think the chances are of us climbing up to that opening?"

Crispin sighed loudly. "Slim to none, and even if one of us could climb like a spider, we would still be stuck in the wrong realm."

I narrowed my eyes at his tone. "Let's can the bad attitude. We're stuck here because of you, after all." I stuffed my growing panic back down as I approached him. "We just need to think. We both got here, we can both get back." I paced across the stone floor of our prison. I could do this. I had traveled once, I could travel again.

Crispin pushed away from the wall he'd been leaning against. "I'm willing to try, but I fear it will be up to you."

I abruptly stopped my pacing to turn on him. "Why is it up to me? I barely just learned to travel myself. I don't know if I can take you with me. We might *both* end up trapped in a star."

He leaned his head back with another heavy sigh. "I was able to use a mixture of magic and alchemy to travel from my homeland to earth. It took considerable power to blaze a new path, but fortunately I had some old star charts to guide me." He lowered his head to look at me. "Then when I reached earth, I found I had far less magic than before. I knew right then and there that I would not be able to travel back on my own. And here —" He spread his arms wide. "Here I feel hardly any magic at all."

I tried to sense what he was talking about, but I really didn't feel much of a difference.

"You are half celestial, Eva." He stepped toward me. "You channel the magic of the stars, and the stars are *everywhere*. Even right up there." He nodded toward the slowly darkening hole in the ceiling.

I took a moment to consider his words. "So let me get this straight. You left the elven realm only to get trapped on earth. Then you risked traveling here, knowing you might not be able to return."

"I didn't mean to actually come here," he huffed. "I was only trying to create a path for you. Something to use as practice." He looked away, then muttered, "Only I made a slight miscalculation."

I crossed my arms. "You know, if we ever get out of here, I'm going to have to seriously reconsider working with you."

His nose wrinkled at my words. "Well, I suppose I couldn't blame you," he said tersely. "Now are you going to try to get us out of here, or not?"

"Considering the alternative is being trapped here for eternity with you," I stepped toward him, "I'm willing to try."

He straightened, then looked down at me as I neared. "Splendid. So what did you do to get here? It seemed like the devil had angered you."

I took a deep breath and let it out. I wasn't sure what to tell him. That my magic came from a mixture of sex and strong emotions? "Sebastian was trying to help me in his own irritating way. And it worked, though perhaps not how he planned." I looked around the room. "Though who knows? Maybe he's just watching, laughing at us."

"While I do not know the extent of his power, this realm might be a bit too far for him to travel."

My eyes whipped to his face. "I thought you said we were close to earth."

"I did. But maybe not quite as close as the hells . . . " he trailed off.

"Wonderful," I muttered.

Maybe Sebastian was capable of rescuing me, and maybe not. Either way, I knew I had to try. I reached out toward Crispin. "Give me your hand."

He looked down at my waiting palm, then up to my face. "Why?"

I extended my hand more forcefully. "Do you want me to try, or not?"

He seemed to think about it for a moment, then he slid his palm over mine.

His skin was warm and dry, but I didn't sense much else from him. My magic had retreated somewhere deep inside me.

"Great," I huffed.

He kept his hand in mine. "What is it?"

"Do you trust me?"

His brows lifted. "Trust you? I only just met you yesterday."

"Well you're going to have to develop some trust real fast." I stepped toward him until our bodies nearly touched.

"What are you doing?"

I gritted my teeth. "Less questions would make this easier."

He watched me wide-eyed for a moment, then his throat bobbed as he swallowed. "Very well."

Gods, I couldn't believe I was going to do this. But I could barely feel my magic. I needed something, or *someone*, to bring it out in me.

I dropped his hand, then placed my palms against his chest, pushing my body against his. I didn't react to him the way I did to Mistral, but I also didn't really know him. My reaction to the others had grown over time.

"It would help if you touched me," I said.

His hands went awkwardly to my waist. "Not that I don't appreciate the invitation—"

My cheeks were already on fire, and it was growing worse by the moment. I forced myself to meet his eyes. "It's weird, I know, but *touch* seems to bring my magic to the surface. It's only happened so far with two high goblins and Sebastian."

His eyebrows shot up.

I gave him a warning look. "And I'm only telling you this to try to help you understand. It might be our only way out of here." I lifted one finger toward his face. "But don't you dare tell anyone else about it."

With his eyebrows still raised, he reluctantly nodded. "You have my word."

"Good. Now kiss me."

He didn't make a move. The light changed again overhead. It would be dark far too soon.

I felt ridiculous after arguing about kissing Gabriel, but for once I was in charge, and it made me feel bold. I took his jaw in my hands, then pulled his lips to mine.

I had never kissed an elf before, and for a moment all I could think was, *Gods, he tastes like springtime.* Then his hands went to my waist, pulling me more firmly against him. He tilted me back, deepening the kiss.

A hint of magic flared within me, reacting to his touch. I could tell he sensed it too when he started to pull away, but my plan was working. We couldn't lose the thin bond I had established.

Instead I pushed him back against a low slab of stone, straddling him, my action surprising even myself. But the magic was growing. I was starting to see stars. I pushed my fingers through his short hair and kissed him for all that I was worth.

My actions seemed to release the rest of his doubt as his hands went to my hips, grinding me against him. The magic built, but I had no direction. No pathway.

The only thing I had to think of was Sebastian's smug face. I pictured him standing in Crispin's tower, laughing at us.

Crispin's hands went under the edge of my shirt, smoothing across my bare waist, then tickling up my lower back. As the magic between us built, I could feel more of him too. Not his body, but the magic buried deep inside. I could practically taste crisp new leaves, and smell the first flowers of spring. I could feel a gentle clear brook flowing over me.

Our magic reached a crescendo and I focused on Sebastian once again. I closed my eyes as I felt the shift, though I could still see stars behind my eyelids. I knew if I opened my eyes, they would be dancing all around us. A wave of dizziness hit me and I broke our kiss, but held tightly to Crispin's shoulders, not wanting to lose him.

We ended up on his work table, tossing aside metal instruments and crinkling papers. I hunched over him, fingers still digging into his shoulders, afraid to move.

A silent moment passed.

"Um, Gorgeous?" Crispin's voice seemed startlingly loud. "Not that I object to this position, but you should be aware that we now have an audience."

I finally opened my eyes, straightening as I still straddled Crispin.

Sebastian tilted his head as he observed us, his smile just as smug as I had imagined. Elena stood a few paces behind him, eyes wide and jaw slack.

I shot off of Crispin so abruptly that I stumbled and nearly fell off the table. He gripped my arm, catching me before I could plummet face first onto the floor.

My cheeks were hot with embarrassment, but it was nothing compared to the relief I felt. I had done it. I had brought us home.

"I'm surprised it took you so long," Sebastian said with a truly evil smile.

I balled my hands into fists as Crispin climbed off the table, taking a moment to readjust his trousers.

"Well, that was bloody brilliant." He turned around, reaching for his journal. He picked up a pen and started scribbling notes haphazardly. "And here I thought I'd be helping you. What an experience."

I stared at him, stunned by his quick recovery. "But I thought you've traveled before?"

He paused his scribbling to look back at me, completely ignoring Sebastian and Elena. "Of course, but with help." He straightened and stepped toward me. "And those stars. I've never seen anything like it."

I frowned, glancing at Sebastian.

"You can speak of it to no one," he said to Crispin, a threat clear in his tone.

Crispin seemed taken aback. "Well obviously. And I did give dear Eva my word." He turned back to his scribbling, a moment later finishing whatever he was writing with a flourish. He turned back around. "Eva, this is amazing. You and I together, we could really figure it out. Not that I don't enjoy the city, but my magic isn't half what it was back home."

"I mostly just want to find my mother," I muttered.

"Yes, yes." Seeming to remember something he had forgotten, he turned back to his notes. "All in due time. I imagine locating your mother will be more simple than returning to my homeland."

I wasn't so sure about that, considering the elven realm would remain in one place while my mother was on the run, but I didn't speak my thoughts out loud. Mostly, I was still just trying to wrap my mind around what I had accomplished. And I was trying to remember just exactly how I had done it.

"I have much to think on today," Crispin continued, not noticing my hesitation. "But I'm sure I can come up with more for tomorrow. Would you be willing to return?" He looked back and forth between me and Sebastian.

Elena had recovered enough to watch me expectantly.

"Sure, I guess." I looked at Sebastian.

He nodded slightly, that infuriating smile still on his face.

Elena beamed at me. "I'll show you both out."

Sebastian turned with her, but Crispin caught my arm before I could follow them.

He lowered his voice, leaning close to my cheek. "You knew what would happen. That's why you kissed me. Has this been happening for long?"

My blush resumed. At this point, my cheeks may as well remain permanently red. "No, not very long."

"But just with the three you mentioned?" His blue eyes flicked toward Sebastian waiting by the door with Elena.

"Yep," I said through gritted teeth. "Just the three I mentioned... And now you."

If the statement made him at all uncomfortable, he didn't show it. "Fascinating." He was already looking back toward his notes. "I'll see you tomorrow."

I watched him turn back toward his work table, the surface now in total disarray from our landing, then I walked toward Sebastian and Elena, shaking my head. The theory of me reacting to people from other worlds could have still applied, if not for Gabriel. Me reacting to strong magic was still a possibility, but now I wasn't even sure if that was true. I hadn't reacted to Crispin at first. Not until we kissed. Not until I had *wanted* it. Like my body had chosen him.

I lowered my gaze as Elena held the door open for us.

The only real conclusion I could come up with was that I was reacting to sexual attraction. Getting hot and heavy brought my magic to the surface, and when the other person had enough magic to meet mine, the stars came out. But it had never happened before. Not until Mistral.

As we walked silently through the stone halls of the palace, I thought about what it all could potentially mean. I had never wanted more power, but if it meant finding my mother and ending the deadly game surrounding her...

I would do whatever it took.

)) ✦ ✦ ✦ ✦ ✦ ((

WE LEFT Elena with another promise to return tomorrow. I was somehow not surprised that Sebastian chose to escort me on the twenty minute walk to my apartment. The silence stretched between us as we left Greengate Park behind, until I couldn't take it anymore and I grabbed Sebastian's collar, hauling him into the nearest alleyway.

I pointed a finger in his face. "You knew. You knew exactly what was going to happen, and what I would have to do to get myself out of there."

"I suspected. Knowing is far different."

His blasé tone made me clench my jaw. "You are such an asshole."

His brow twitched. "I'm not sure why you're angry. I'm helping you more than anyone else."

He kept saying that, but I wasn't sure that word meant what he thought it meant. "As we've already established, you're helping yourself. And you better not go back on what you said. When I find my mom, we're not turning her in. We'll use her to find whoever created the bounty." It was actually starting to feel like a reality that I would find my mother. Finally. After all this time. But part of me wondered if I might be dooming her in doing so.

Sebastian tilted his head. "Will we?"

I inhaled sharply, but he laughed before I could say anything else. Once he had control of himself, he gave me a humoring smile. "As I've told you, the payment of my debt is in the acquisition of the object. I don't care how you get it. And I don't care what happens to your mother."

And neither should I, the words cut through my thoughts. I knew I shouldn't care, but I did. "Okay, we will figure out how to get the... object. Tomorrow. For now, I have other places to be."

He leaned back against the brick wall behind him and crossed his arms. "Like the Bogs?"

"Yeah, so what?"

He pushed away from the wall, stepping close.

"What are you doing?" I started to pull back, but he grabbed my waist, pulling me forcefully against him.

Before I could react, his lips met mine. He kissed

me deeply enough that his dark magic seemed to touch every part of me. And without thinking, I was kissing him too, my arms limp with latent indecision at my sides. I started to see stars again, and I found myself lifting my arms, pressing against him, hungry for more. My body throbbed with need, making me wish we weren't in a public place, though I was lucky we were.

He broke the kiss, leaving me panting. "You can do as you wish with Mistral," he murmured. "But remember, your contract is with me." He pulled me close again, his lips grazing mine, his dark magic tugging at my core. "And remember," he said with his mouth near mine. "You are granting him power too."

"Is that what you want then?" I asked breathlessly. "Power?"

"Of course." Still holding me close, he trailed a kiss across my neck, making my body tight with arousal. "But at least I'm upfront about it." He disappeared in a flash of black, leaving me to regain my balance *and* my composure in the secluded alleyway.

I inhaled sharply, then let it out, my skin still tingling from his touch. It simply was *not* fair how I reacted to him. Next time he tried to kiss me...

My thoughts trailed off. What made me think there would be a next time? I knew Games was toying with me, but the offer was still there. And as infuriating as it was, part of me wanted to take it.

But that part was an idiot, and she needed to shut up.

Shaking my head, I tugged my shirt straight and marched back out to the street. I would go home to grab a few things, then I would catch a cab to the Bogs. After what happened with Crispin, I knew I had to explore things further. I had two goblins who I was pretty sure were willing to try, and neither of them would try to steal my soul.

I slid a hand into my pocket to make sure I still had my apartment key, but came out with a crumpled piece of paper. I unfolded it to find an address and a time, 10 AM. The handwriting was the same as the previous note.

I lowered it, looking around the street as people walked to and fro, not paying me any mind. I hadn't seen Lucas this time, so I knew it wasn't from him. And I doubted it was Sebastian or one of the elves. So who?

I didn't know the exact address, but I recognized the street. Given the location, it was probably a restaurant, or at least a relatively safe public place.

I double checked the time again, then shoved the note back into my pocket. I had until tomorrow morning to decide if I would go, but deep down I knew my curiosity would get the better of me.

It usually did.

10

Gabriel held me tightly against him as the horse's hooves thundered beneath us. Ringo was buried down in my messenger bag with a handful of potato chips for the ride. There would be crumbs everywhere, but I hadn't been able to say no when he spotted the bag of chips in a convenience store window. The stars overhead were mostly obscured by dense gray clouds, and I could already smell the rain. Hopefully we would make it to the Citadel before the moisture started to fall.

Gabriel's deep voice sounded near my ear. "Letting a devil into one's realm is unheard of. They must have had ulterior motives."

I hadn't told him about the first note I'd received, nor the second for that matter. For a moment, I debated letting it slip, but he seemed to be worrying about me more than enough already. "I already told you. The motive was to save Crispin."

"You did that without Sebastian's help."

I had already told him pretty much everything else, including kissing Crispin. I knew it would come out eventually, so may as well get it over with. "You really think Crispin would trap himself in a parallel realm just to get me to kiss him?"

The horse slowed as we neared Mistral's estate. "I would not put it past him," Gabriel muttered.

Even though we had discussed my kiss with Crispin, we had not yet discussed our own kiss, as was evident by the sudden tension in the air between us.

Gabriel slid off the horse then lifted me down like usual, but this time, he didn't release me.

I looked up into his dark eyes.

"You need to be careful, Eva. Did my warning truly mean nothing to you?"

I lowered my gaze. "It's not like I've really had a choice in anything. Can't you understand how insane this all has been for me?"

His hands flexed around my waist, his fingertips nearly touching at the small of my back. The sensation made me shiver. Made me want to move closer.

"Yes, I can understand that." He leaned down toward my face. "But Eva, you must also understand. You already feel different to me. Different from only yesterday. Others will notice."

I stiffened. Sebastian had said the same thing. Had Crispin already noticed something? Did he trap himself on purpose to lure me into saving him? I found myself not wanting to meet Gabriel's eyes, so I looked at his mouth instead, which wasn't much better as I instantly flashed back on our kiss. "If I don't learn to travel to find my mom, everyone's going to be after me anyways. I need to put an end to this."

He waited until I finally looked up at him. "Let *us* be the ones to help you."

My throat went tight. "*Us?*"

He didn't look away.

"You mean, you want to..."

"We should go inside," he said softly.

He finally released me, then led the way toward the entrance. His horse waited obediently behind us. I wasn't sure if Gabriel would return to tend to it, or if someone else would. I supposed it wasn't really my problem.

Ringo popped his head out of my bag to look up at me as I trailed after Gabriel.

What the hell was that? I mouthed, darting my eyes up toward Gabriel's back ahead of us.

Ringo shrugged his little shoulders.

Shaking my head, I followed Gabriel inside. *Let us help you,* he'd said, almost as if they already had a plan. Part of me wanted to run away. But I found a bigger part of me would never forgive myself for not at least learning what might be in store.

I scooped another forkful of blueberry pie into my mouth. It was delicious, and exactly what I needed. That, and Mistral's calm reaction to learning what happened with Crispin.

Though Mistral sat at the dining table with me, he had only a glass of wine. Gabriel sat across from me, to Mistral's right on the other side of the table.

The high goblin beside me sipped his wine, gray eyes thoughtful. "It is curious that Crispin would end up in a pocket realm like that. No dangers, where he could wait as long as was needed for Eva to save him."

I stabbed my fork into my pie, leaving it sticking upright. "I really didn't get the impression that he was trying to manipulate me. I don't think he's interested in that sort of thing, or in the game. He's entirely consumed with his research."

I had already considered Crispin's reaction to the kiss. He had seemed more excited about the possibilities for discovery than anything else. Completely absorbed in his own little world, was Crispin.

"And Princess Millelena?" Mistral continued. "How did she react?"

I glowered, tired of being questioned about it. "Shocked, then hopeful. I really do think her intentions are pure. And she believes the Realm Breaker is a myth. Her interest in me stems from Sebastian's belief that I can actually find my mother in another realm."

We all turned at the sound of footsteps, my body

suddenly tense since I so rarely witnessed other goblins in Mistral's estate.

A young man with deep brown hair and green eyes peeked his head in through the open doorway. His eyes widened for a moment as he observed me, then they darted to Mistral. "Forgive me, my Lord, but it's Even-lee. It's happening again."

Mistral's expression shut down as I looked to him for an explanation. He stood. "You'll need to stay here, Eva. Please make yourself at home." He strode toward the doorway.

I stood and grabbed Gabriel's arm before he could follow Mistral. "I don't think so. If you guys are involved in all my troubles, I get to be involved in yours. Tell me what's going on." I pictured Mistral, barely able to stand, his clothing mud-streaked. I knew this must have something to do with what had happened then.

I dug my fingers into Gabriel's arm, making it clear that I would not be letting go.

Mistral and Gabriel shared a long look. The messenger seemed like he would rather be *anywhere* else.

Finally, Mistral nodded, his eyes still on Gabriel. "Keep her safe." He turned on his heel, walking out the doorway with the messenger scurrying after him.

"Come," Gabriel ordered, his expression dark. Any hint of the softness he had shown me earlier was gone. Every inch of him looked like a rugged warrior once more.

I suddenly regretted my decision, but I grabbed Ringo from the chair where he was hiding, then followed Gabriel out into the hall. We went down the stairs like we were headed toward the front entrance, but before we could reach it, Gabriel veered off down another hall.

We went into a bed chamber lit only by a single lantern, the color warm like candlelight, though no flame flickered within. The space was bare bones, just a simple bed, dresser, and a small bookshelf. Was this his bedroom? Compared to where I usually stayed, I would think he would have chosen somewhere nicer.

He reached for something in the shadows leaning near the bed, then stepped back, revealing a sword nearly as tall as I was. He strapped it across his back, the leather-wrapped hilt poking over his shoulder.

My jaw fell open at the sight of the sword. "What exactly are we heading into?"

"It's just a precaution." He finally turned to face me, his eyes glinting in the lantern light. "Goblin magic isn't entirely suited to this realm. Sometimes it gets out of hand. I cannot tell you what we might find." He eyed me steadily. "It's not too late for you to stay here." His eyes lowered. "At the very least, I recommend you leave *that* behind."

I looked down at Ringo trembling in my hands. "What do you want to do?"

He trembled harder, seeming too afraid to answer.

"He has seen the imbalances before," Gabriel explained. "Leave him."

I walked him over to Gabriel's bed, then set him on a pillow. "I'll be back for you soon, okay?"

Ringo lifted up the edge of the blanket, then scurried underneath it, forming a small, trembling ball. I followed Gabriel out of the room, shutting the door behind me.

"I didn't mean for you to leave him with all of my things," he said lowly.

"He won't do anything bad!" I left Ringo alone with all of *my* things all the time.

"He is still a goblin, Eva," Gabriel sighed. "Do not forget that."

I wasn't sure exactly what he meant, but didn't have time to think about it as he hurried me forward. Once we were outside, we headed toward the stables. I didn't see his horse anywhere, so someone else must have taken care of it since he had never left my sight.

We found his horse in a stall amid other snuffling beasts. Most of them looked mostly horse like, but some had peculiar colors and shapes. I would have loved to observe them more closely, but Gabriel put a hand at the small of my back as he opened his horse's stall.

His huge horse walked out obediently, not seeming put out to be disturbed again so quickly. Before I could react, Gabriel tossed me onto the horse's back.

My hands met silky fur and warmth. "Aren't we forgetting the saddle?"

"No time." He vaulted up behind me, wrapping an arm around my waist, pulling me snug against him.

"But what about the bridle?" My voice came out more shrill than I would have liked.

"No time," he said again.

His heels patted the horse's sides and it took off like a bolt out the open stable gate. Gabriel leaned forward, sheltering my back with his broad chest and caging me with his arms.

I fought the urge to shriek, knowing I just had to trust him as the cool wind bit into my cheeks and the scenery passed by much faster than I had previously experienced.

Definitely *not* the evening I'd had in mind.

11

As we rode, Gabriel explained that Evenlee was the village we had visited together. Other than that, there wasn't much he could tell me. We would simply have to see for ourselves what had the messenger so worried.

The first thing I noticed as we neared was that the village was dark, save for a cluster of goblins holding torches. Then I realized that they hadn't actually turned out the lights. Their homes were covered in thick swarming masses of vines. There were so many vines that they completely covered the windows, blocking out all light.

And there weren't enough goblins standing out in the road. Some of them had to be trapped inside the homes. Sure enough, when our horse stilled and we stopped to listen, I could hear shouting and banging coming from inside the nearest structures, the noise muffled by the stone and thick vines.

"What happened?" I gasped.

Gabriel gripped me tightly against him, making sure I stayed on the horse. I glanced back at him, then followed his gaze further into the village where Mistral stood on his own. The huddled goblins were watching him too.

"Stay on the horse," Gabriel ordered. "If you feel you are in danger, just kick your feet. She knows the way home."

I gripped his arm before he could dismount, stupidly hung up on the fact that I would have assumed such a massive horse was male. I hadn't taken a close enough look to tell one way or another. "I'm not just going to leave you guys. Tell me what's going on so I can help."

"This has nothing to do with you, Eva." He pulled his arm free from mine, then dismounted, marching off toward Mistral.

I felt uneasy as soon as he was gone, having no faith in my ability to control the massive beast, though it didn't make a move in any direction. Some of the goblins were now looking my way, muttering amongst themselves.

I cast a furtive glance at them, then turned my head to watch Gabriel as he drew that massive sword, approaching Mistral. They were too far for me to hear what words were exchanged between them, but they both watched as the vines trailed ever higher. Some of the homes were nothing but green, completely sealing away whoever was inside.

It was magic, but it didn't feel like bad magic. I could sense it emanating from the nearest vines, but it just felt like the Bogs. Only *amplified.* I remembered what Gabriel had said about the magic getting out of control, and I realized this is what he meant. It took goblin magic to create the Bogs, but here, it seemed like it was... unraveling.

Sword drawn, Gabriel watched Mistral's back as the other man sank to his knees, placing his hands against the dirt. I felt a stronger flare of magic just as it hit some of the vines, making them retreat. They were still for a moment, making the muttering from the other goblins seem loud, then they abruptly resumed their climb, leaves slithering and hissing across stone.

I felt another pulse of magic, and realized it was Mistral pouring more magic into the ground, trying to control the vines. Was this what Sebastian had meant? Was this the bargain Mistral had struck with him? I didn't see how else he could have enough power to actually control the land.

I found myself slipping from the horse without thinking. I had taken several steps toward Mistral and Gabriel without realizing what I was doing. I stopped, glancing at the gathered goblins now that half of them were watching me.

A larger pulse of magic made my legs go temporarily numb, then the vines retreated further, and this time their retreat continued. I whipped my gaze in Mistral's direction to see him lowering further to the ground.

Gabriel looked back at me, his eyes shining in the dark. Seeing that I was off the horse, he shook his head.

Behind him, Mistral slumped onto his side, drawing Gabriel's attention.

With the other goblins whispering desperately behind me, I ran toward them. Something was wrong. *Very* wrong.

Gabriel held out an arm to bar my way as I reached them. "Don't touch him."

I looked down at Mistral, but I couldn't see his face through his hair. He had managed to climb to his knees, but it seemed he could go no further.

I inhaled a trembling breath. "He can't maintain it. He doesn't have enough magic within him." As soon as I spoke the words, I knew they were true. The land was powerful, and so much of that power was surging up through the vines. Mistral's own magic was like a flickering candle next to a forest fire.

"You can sense it?" Gabriel's voice was strained. He was worried.

"I don't know who wouldn't sense it." The waves of magic had been impressive, but it wasn't enough. The vines were beginning to stir again, ready to resume their climb. They hadn't lowered enough to reveal any of the doors or windows of the homes. I remembered the village as it was. The goblins seated under glowing lanterns. The tavern a lovely warm place filled with laughter.

I had to do something,

I tried to go to Mistral, but Gabriel held me back.

"You have to let me help him."

He gripped my arm, trying to shove me behind him. "It's too dangerous."

"It's too dangerous not to." I tried to tug away from him. I didn't have enough magical knowledge to know exactly what was happening, but I sensed Mistral at our feet. He was fading. And that was all I needed to know.

"Someone has to help him." I tried tugging away again. "If you won't let me, then you need to do it."

He turned his gaze down to me, and it was filled with pain. He understood what was happening, probably better than I did, and I understood in that moment that he couldn't help. He didn't have whatever Sebastian had given to Mistral in their bargain.

I met that pain-filled gaze solidly. "Let me go, Gabriel."

His hand released me reflexively.

I met his eyes for a moment longer, feeling sympathy for the indecision I saw there. But there was no time to offer him any comfort. I dropped to my knees beside Mistral, hovering one hand over him, afraid to actually touch him.

When he didn't even seem to notice my presence, I laid my hand on his shoulder. Still, nothing happened. I could feel his tenuous control as he tried to hold the vines back.

I wanted to help, but now that I was here, I had no idea what to do.

I lifted my hand to move his hair out of the way, placing my bare palm against his neck. His skin was cold. I could barely feel his pulse.

Sebastian claimed I had given Mistral new magic, but I felt no hint of it now. The vines didn't move. Nothing moved. Even the onlookers had fallen silent.

"Tell me how to help you," I muttered, keeping my hand pressed against his neck, willing some of that warm magic to flare between us.

He inhaled sharply, startling me, then he lifted one hand to push my palm more firmly against his neck. A tiny spark of my magic came to life within me.

I sank to the ground beside him and he finally met my eyes. He didn't speak, but the look was enough. Whatever he was trying to do, it was too much. He couldn't control the land. He couldn't keep the goblin realm as it was on his own.

A faint glow began to emanate from my skin where it touched him. A prickle of magic. "What do you need me to do?"

"Just, trust me." His words were so weak I barely heard them.

Panic spiked through me. *Trust me.* They weren't words I usually responded well to. The only person I could really trust was Braxton.

He slumped a little further to the ground.

Waves of panic crashed through my body, but I took a deep breath to quiet them. He had never offered me actual harm, and he had comforted me when I needed it. I hadn't known him long, but he had already proven that he could be there for me in ways that few others could.

"I trust you," I breathed, even though it felt like a strange sort of sacrifice to do so.

He gripped my palm tightly against him for a moment, then used my hand to pull me toward him, surprisingly fiercely. I ended up on the ground beneath him as he laid himself over me.

I looked up at him wide-eyed, my breath catching in my throat, then he kissed me, and the magic spiked between us.

As soon as our lips met, I understood what he was doing. We had raised a lot of magic between us before. Maybe enough magic to control the land.

I relaxed into the kiss, my body reacting to the feel of him on top of me, then I remembered the goblin onlookers and stiffened.

I broke the kiss, turning my head toward the onlookers, but all I could see was Gabriel standing with his back to us a few paces away.

"No one will come near," Mistral said into my ear. He lifted himself to look down at me, though his arms were trembling.

"I know." I spoke past the lump in my throat.

"If you are not able to do this, then speak the truth."

I turned my head to meet those stunning gray eyes. "What will happen to you if I can't?"

He met my eyes, but didn't answer, because he could only speak the truth. And he knew if he did, that I wouldn't want to say no.

With a new sense of resolve, I lifted my hands to cradle his chin, pulling him down on top of me. "Gabriel better keep them *far* away." I kissed him, and this time with abandon.

He sank against me as I wrapped my legs around him, pressing my back into the damp grass. He kissed down my neck, and more power flared with every caress. It was easier this time, like it was waiting just below the surface.

Just like with Crispin—

I silenced my thoughts, not wanting to get distracted from our task, which became easy as Mistral reached a hand between us to unbutton my jeans. The tug at my waistband sent a tug even lower, pleasure already building even though all we had done was kiss.

"I do hate to rush," he whispered against my skin, "but I can't hold the land for much longer."

If he thought he needed to apologize, he was wrong, because the idea of skipping frantically to the finale had its own appeal to me. He ground against me, and I could feel him hard and ready through his pants.

"Do what you need to do," I panted.

The next thing I knew, he had flipped me over and

pulled my jeans down from my ass. I felt him reaching into his pocket, then shifting to lower his pants with the crinkle of foil. I had a moment to remember that we were once again not alone, then Mistral slid inside me with a single thrust.

I let out a moan then cut myself off, glancing in Gabriel's direction, but I could only see the silhouette of his back, and no sign of the goblins beyond. Mistral pulled almost out of me, then thrust again, slamming against my body.

The pleasure already building in my core exploded. I pushed my fingers through the grass, pressing my cheek against the damp blades, breathing in the heady scent of fertile soil. Magic built up in my chest as Mistral pounded against me, but I wasn't sure what to do with it. This time, I had no need to be anywhere else.

He thrust harder, making me groan every time his body met mine, bringing me close to the edge. "How do I—"

He leaned his chest over my back, the change in angle making me gasp. "Just let go, Eva. Just let your magic go. I will guide it."

Mistral ground himself into me, making my body tense around him, dead suddenly all I could see were stars. But I didn't go anywhere. I could still feel his hands on my hips. I could feel him thrusting into me, pressing my knees into the cold grass and soil, dampening my jeans still wrapped around my legs. I did as he asked, I relaxed into the sensations, loosening my grip on my magic, letting it flow around us.

And just like that, it poured into him. Even with my eyes closed and concentration, the starlight was almost blinding. An orgasm hit me, and with it I cried out and let loose my final shred of control. I could feel the spell he wove together, sending it into the earth, asserting dominance over all that wild magic.

But some of that magic refused to be tamed. And it called out not to him, but to me. I felt it gripping me. I tried to steady myself, but I was still seeing stars. I could sense the shift, but I couldn't see any way to stop it.

And when I opened my eyes, I was entirely alone.

I SAT BOLT UPRIGHT, looking around frantically. One of my feet had ended up in the water, soaking through my sneaker and chilling me further. I yanked it out of the stream with a hiss, and struggled to pull up and fasten my jeans. Once I was fully clothed, I glanced around warily. I had no idea where I'd ended up, but it still *felt* like the Bogs.

Which was good and bad. Good, because maybe I wasn't far from Gabriel and Mistral, but bad because things like trolls roamed the Bogs, and I was defenseless.

I had only taken a few steps when something splashed in the water behind me. I whirled around, lifting my hands defensively for what good it would do me, then blinked down at a stunningly gorgeous woman with green tinged skin so pale it picked up the moonlight. She smiled at me, showing perfect white teeth, no fangs.

"Um, hello," I said hesitantly.

She rose further out of the water, revealing that she was nude, though it didn't make me feel any better. I knew a goblin woman lurking in a stream waiting for an unsuspecting visitor would not be defenseless. She tilted her head, splaying dark, wet locks across her shoulders. "Hello. Are you lost?"

I took another step away from the water. That was not a question you answered honestly in the Bogs. "Nope, just waiting for a couple of very powerful high goblins to meet me."

She took another step, rising further to reveal her slender form. "I don't see nor hear any goblins coming this way." Her words held a distinct *hiss*, her voice breathy.

I stepped back again, bumping against a tree. "Trust me, they'll be here."

I flinched at another splash as a second woman popped above the water's surface. With her face dripping, she smiled at me, though her words were for her companion. "She shines like the moon, doesn't she?"

The other woman tilted her head. "More like the stars. Where did you come from, little star?"

Her bare feet had reached the bank. I wasn't sure

how fast she could move on land, but I had no intention of finding out.

"I'll just wait for my companions… somewhere else." I stepped around the tree behind me, prepared to turn and run, but as soon as I turned my way was blocked.

A third woman, dripping with water, regarded me from only inches away. She was older and plumper than the other two, and standing close enough that I could see her eyes were the deep aqua of a distant ocean. "You smell like goblin magic. How odd."

I staggered back as she reached for me, bumping into the same tree I'd stepped around. Green tinted hands reached around each side of the trunk, grabbing my arms and locking me in place against the rough bark. Serene stars watched from overhead, offering me no help at all.

The eldest of the trio stepped close again, her eyes dancing with mischief. "Would you like to learn to swim, little star?"

I tugged against the hands holding me, but I couldn't budge them. Even when I shifted slightly, they didn't let go. "Gabriel!" I shouted, having no idea if he was near enough to hear me. "Mistral!"

No answer. But they had to be looking for me. They wouldn't just leave me out here alone. Every time I was in the Bogs, Gabriel always found me.

The goblin woman in front of me darted her hand toward my face, then knotted her fingers in my hair near my scalp. She wrenched my head painfully to one side. "Let's see if stars can breathe underwater. Maybe before she dies, she'll sparkle for us."

The other two women laughed somewhere behind me.

I pulled against the grip on my hair, but she was just as strong as the one holding me around the tree. "What did I ever do to you!" I gasped at the stabbing pain in my head.

The one behind the tree released me, then the one holding my hair yanked me hard enough that I lost my footing. She started dragging me across the ground toward the water. "Little star shined too brightly."

I gripped her slick hand around my hair, trying to right myself. "Gabriel!" He had to be coming. He always found me.

Water splashed around me as the woman dragged me into the stream. It was ice cold, stealing my breath. She tugged me across the surface, then plunged me downward, putting my head under. I thrashed against her, unable to feel the pain in my scalp with the ice cold water making my skin go numb. My final breath whooshed out of me in the stream of bubbles, the grip on my hair unrelenting.

Panic struck straight to my heart. No one was coming to save me, and curse it all, I was not going to die like this. I had managed to travel to Sebastian just by thinking of him, and I could do it again. I didn't need someone else to call out my magic. Just as I was about to black out, I pictured Gabriel standing over me. He was far too tall and bossy, but he would protect me. I knew he would.

Lights sparkled around me, stars underwater. The woman yanked on my head, tugging me deeper, then suddenly her hand was gone. The stream and icy cold were gone too.

I landed hard on dry ground, coughing up water.

"Eva!"

I felt hands on me. *Big* hands. Gabriel gripped my shoulders, helping me sit upright. I tried to look at him, but water streamed from my hair into my eyes.

He pushed it out of my face so I could see him. He knelt before me, his horse a few paces behind him. "Gods, Eva, you can't just go disappearing like that."

"It's not like I did it on—" I started choking, coughing up more stream water.

He held onto me until my choking fit was over, but now I was trembling. It wasn't a warm night, and my clothes were soaking wet.

Before I could say another word, Gabriel lifted me into his arms.

"The village?" I managed to ask as he carried me toward his horse.

"Under control. Everyone is safe, for now."

I huddled against him for warmth, pushing my wet hair out of my face again. "It's too much for Mistral to manage. He can't keep it up." I didn't understand everything, but I knew that much. My teeth started chattering and I buried my cheek against his chest.

Reaching his horse, he looked down at me. "I know. And he knows it too."

"Sebastian told me about their bargain," I chattered. "I know that Mistral took control of the land once his mother died." And I was starting to suspect something else. Something terrible. "It killed her, didn't it?"

He met my waiting gaze. "Many of the creatures here cannot survive without the Bogs."

"Is it worth Mistral dying over?"

"He seems to think so." He lifted me onto the horse, then boosted himself up behind me.

"Well he's wrong," I muttered.

His arms wrapped around me, pulling me close. "At least we finally agree on something."

12

WE MET Mistral back at the village. He and the other goblins had fanned out, searching for me. Gabriel helped me down from his horse as a few of them gathered around us, and I found myself unable to meet anyone's eyes.

Just how much had they seen?

Judging by the way they watched me, quite a lot.

Mistral put an arm around me, pulling me close. "You're shivering. What happened? You disappeared into thin air."

I glanced at the gathered goblins. "Maybe we should talk about that later."

His hollow eyes widened briefly. It seemed that even with my help, fighting against the vines had taken everything he had. "Yes, of course."

I looked at the surrounding buildings. Not a vine in sight. "So it's safe now?"

"For now," Gabriel muttered at my back.

One of the other goblins finally got brave enough to step forward. She had short auburn hair and olive skin, her eyes large and brown. She wrung her hands, then smoothed the skirt of her simple white dress now stained with dirt. "We wanted to thank you," she said to me. "We know you helped save us, and you didn't have to. Perhaps the tales the old ones tell about celestials are misguided."

I wrinkled my nose. "No, they're probably true, but I'm not a full celestial. Either way, you're welcome."

She seemed a little confused by my response, but she accepted it with a curtsy, then scurried back toward the others. The rest of the villagers were hesitantly entering their homes, some walking around them to assess damage caused by the heavy vines.

I gripped Mistral's arm as we watched them. "We *really* need to talk."

"I thought you might say that."

I glanced back at Gabriel, exchanging a knowing look. I knew it wasn't really my business, but something had to be done. Without my help, someone might have died tonight. Perhaps many someones. I realized for the first time that finding the Realm Breaker wasn't just about Mistral going home.

He hadn't lied. He did want to go, but I was pretty sure he wanted to take all of the Bogs with him.

With my only clothing soaked through with river water, I ended up in the softest robe I had ever experienced. The burgundy fabric was lightweight, but tightly woven, and I sank into it as I curled up in a chair beside the fire with a cup of tea. The scent of chamomile and honey wafted up toward my face.

Mistral sat in the chair across from mine. Gabriel had excused himself to bring Ringo from his room to mine, but I knew it was just to give us privacy.

Quiet moments ticked by, until finally Mistral asked, "How much did Sebastian tell you?"

I lifted one shoulder, keeping both hands wrapped around my mug of tea. I was perfectly warm now, but keeping my hands on my mug would stop me from fidgeting. "He told me there was a bargain after your mother died. And now you can't leave the Bogs."

"Did he tell you why he did it?"

I shook my head.

"He thought I wouldn't be able to handle it. He thought I would die."

My fingers flexed around my mug. I knew Sebastian was a jerk, but— "He wouldn't do it just to watch you die. He would only go to the trouble if it would benefit him. What would he stand to gain from your death?"

Mistral lowered his chin in acknowledgment. "I see you've come to know him quite well. You are right. Although he did not share his ulterior motives with me, I knew there must be something motivating him. The only possibility I have come up with is that he hoped once I was dead, the magic of the Bogs would be his for the taking."

I lifted my brows. This wasn't even what we were supposed to be talking about, but I was dying to know more. "What would he do with it?"

"You mean you don't know?"

I frowned, then shook my head.

"Sebastian doesn't have enough power to return to the hells. He's just as trapped as the rest of us. Every contract he makes is an attempt to gain power, enough power to travel back-and-forth as he pleases."

"But he pops around like nobody's business." I waved my hand in the air. "How can he do that, but not have enough power to go home?"

"How can you shift in this realm, and even to nearby pocket realms, but not have the power to reach your mother?"

I considered his words, and everything they meant. Realizing something, I set my tea aside and moved to stand. "That bastard told me he could have rescued me when I got stuck with Crispin!"

"You may wish to run off and shout at him, but I assure you it will do you no good."

Gritting my teeth, I lowered back down to my seat. "What a jerk."

One corner of his mouth ticked up. "I will not argue with you on that point."

"Okay," I settled back against my cushions, "so we have established that Sebastian is a monumental asshole who made a bargain to bind you to the Bogs so he could watch you die and steal the wild magic here. But why did you do it? What would have happened if you just let it go?"

"The boundary had been created. We would have lasted for a while. But it would have been like what you saw tonight. Goblin magic is *wild* magic. In my realm, my people work *with* the land. But here... sometimes it works against us. My mother was exceedingly powerful, but eventually it wore her down."

"She died because of it," I finished for him.

Once again, he lowered his chin.

"And now you'll die because of it."

His expression darkened. "Perhaps. But my only other choice is to let my people die instead."

Everything finally clicked into place. Exactly what was at stake, and why Mistral had joined the game. "You don't just want the Realm Breaker to go home. You need it to save your life, and everyone else's."

Again, that slight nod.

"And I have a contract to either give it to a devil, or to give him my own mother."

"A rather unfortunate conundrum."

I studied his face, the firelight rimming the edge of his jaw in soft yellow. "Do you believe that a celestial destroyed the paths to the other realms?"

He was quiet for a moment, watching my face before he finally answered, "I believe it's a possibility. The other option is that we came here and did not have enough magic to go back. Which is true, we are... *less* here. But what has stopped others from coming through? Why have no new goblins arrived to see why we did not return?"

My jaw fell open. It was so obvious, and I had never actually considered it. "But Crispin. He came here."

"He can forge his own temporary paths, as you witnessed today." He glanced back at the dark window. "Or perhaps it is now yesterday."

I slumped further in my seat. Had that really been less than twenty-four hours ago? So much had happened, it felt like an entire week had passed in a single day. "Okay, one last question, then I seriously need to go to sleep."

He quietly waited for me to continue.

"What happened earlier tonight? How were you able to use my magic to control the vines?"

He smiled softly. "Dear Eva, aren't you aware? Celestial magic is the wildest magic of all."

My breath sighed out of me. There was still so much I didn't understand, but my thoughts were continuously dragged back to one single thing. "Whatever magic is growing inside of me, I can't fight it. I have to let it come. If my mother is in a near realm, I am one of the only people who can find her. Either me, another celestial, or maybe someone like Crispin. I don't know why I've reacted to you or the others so strongly, but I have to explore it."

Again, that slight dip of his chin. "I will help you in

whatever way I can. After tonight, I owe you everything. I owe you my life."

His words struck me like a bolt to the chest, because
I knew he meant them. He could only speak the truth to
me. He really felt like he owed me everything.

Earlier, I had agreed to trust him. And deep down, I
did. He had been added to the very short list of people I
actually trusted. He had told me the truth of his situation, and he deserved the same in return.

I leaned forward in my seat. "Recently I received
two separate mysterious notes. I have no idea who
they're from, but I'm going to meet with them
tomorrow."

13

I HELD the crumpled paper up in front of my face, comparing the address with the small diner across the street from me. The curtains were all drawn in the windows to block out the unusually sunny day, but I had watched several people coming and going, and a neon *Open* sign glowed on one side of the glass doors.

It seemed safe enough, and if it wasn't, I had back up. Not only was Ringo in my messenger bag, but Gabriel was loitering further down the street. He looked far too good leaning against the brick wall, white button up undone at the top just so, contrasting with his brown skin. Sunglasses shielded his eyes, the lenses as dark as his hair, which was currently tied back away from his face.

"You're staring, Eva," a small voice whispered below me.

I glanced down at Ringo peeking out of my bag,

143

lifting a brow at him. "Can you really blame me?" My eyes shifted in Gabriel's direction.

Ringo simply stared back at me. He picked up on banter at the strangest of times, but apparently now was not one of those times.

Shaking my head, I crossed the street. There were a few other goblins loitering about, including Gladiola, the woman who had rescued me from the Circus. I spotted her at the next crosswalk, and gave her a subtle nod as I approached the diner.

I opened the door, pulling against the slight suction from the air conditioner inside. There was an open expanse of bar-style seating, the long counter rimmed with several strips of vibrant color. A few people sat there on tall stools, none of them glancing my way. Observing the *seat yourself* sign, I went for a vinyl booth along the wall near the door.

Not long after I sat, a waiter took my coffee order then hurried away. I wiped my sweaty palms on my jeans, then straightened my loose green flannel over my tank-top, anxious to get the meeting over with. I was supposed to return to Emerald Heights today, but whoever had left the note didn't think I should trust the elves. I needed to learn exactly why that was. And I needed to learn it *before* Sebastian found me. I had left his calling card in my apartment when Gabriel took me home to change, but I had a feeling that even without it, it wouldn't be long before he strode through the diner doors.

The waiter returned with my coffee, giving me a tired look when I said I would wait on ordering food. As soon as he turned away, I slipped a sugar packet into my messenger bag for Ringo. I was pretty sure by now that the little guy could subsist entirely on potatoes and sweets.

I glanced around the diner, growing more anxious by the moment. When my watch buzzed on my wrist, I jumped. I looked down at it, seeing Braxton's number, then pushed a button to answer the call.

"Hey Eva, sorry it took me so long to check in."

"I was beginning to wonder if you'd thought better of having such a risky roommate and decided to live in the country."

Braxton laughed. "Not quite, but speaking of your *issues*, that's why I'm calling. I think you might want to come out here."

I turned the volume down on my watch and held it closer to my face. "What? Why? Not that I couldn't use a vacation, but—"

"I know I wasn't supposed to tell anyone what's going on with you, but you know how my mom is."

I pinched my brow and shook my head. "Braxton—"

"She told me some stuff, Eva. Stuff your dad told her right before he died."

My stomach fell to my feet. "What kind of stuff?"

"I think you should just come out here and talk to her in person. You should be safe with the pack around. Plus, she misses you."

I looked up as the diner door opened and I recognized a familiar petite form. "I have to go, Braxton. But I'll think about it, okay?"

"Do more than think about it. I'll get the guest room ready for you." He hung up before I could.

I lowered my wrist to my lap as the woman who had entered the diner approached me. I recognized her instantly. I had committed her appearance to memory, even though we'd only had one conversation.

The celestial woman from the Circus smiled down at me. "I wasn't sure that you'd come. The devil seems to have you completely wrapped up in his scheme."

"Well, I'm here. Although I'm confused at what point you slipped me those two different notes."

Her wide mouth curled into a charming smile, crinkling the skin around her large dark eyes. Her brown hair was so thick it was like a pelt falling all the way down to her waist, blanketing her diaphanous purple blouse. "Yes, I'm rather adept at slipping about unnoticed." She used her body to shield her hand as she wiggled her fingers, sending off a few tiny stars. "I'm Marcie, by the way. We were interrupted the other night before I could introduce myself."

She slid into the other side of the booth, looking harmless. *Yeah right.* She was a pure blooded celestial working with my mom. I wanted to trust her, but she was also connected to Lucas, who had been ordered to kill night runners. I couldn't trust *anyone* who would murder strangers so blatantly.

The waiter returned, and Marcie ordered a hot green tea.

Figured. "Why did you ask me here?"

"I wanted to warn you to stop searching for your mother."

I narrowed my eyes. "And what makes you think I'm still searching for her?"

"Let's see," she tilted her head, draping that long hair all around her, "a powerful devil haunts your every step, you have the protection of the elf king himself, and you have been spending quite a bit of time in the Bogs." She gave me a knowing look.

"None of that means anything."

"Eva, if you find your mother, you're going to get her killed. Don't you realize that all of these men around you just want to turn her in for the bounty? I know she left you, but do you really want to see her dead?"

"That depends. Does she want to see *me* dead?"

She rolled her eyes. "I thought you understood that was an accident. Your mother believed you were already dead."

I stiffened, my mouth going dry. "What?"

I had to wait on an answer as the waiter returned with her tea, then looked expectantly at us for a food order. Marcie stared back at him, deadpan, until he lifted his hands and strode away.

She turned her attention back to me. "Your mother thought you were dead, Evelyn."

"It's Eva," I snapped.

"Yes," she sighed. "Your name change did add to the illusion that you were deceased. She is, of course, thrilled that you are still alive, but you understand why she cannot meet with you."

"No, actually I don't."

She put her hands flat on the table, leaning forward. "These men are using you, Eva. Especially the devil, but the goblins and the elves too. They will see your mother dead."

"They will not," I snapped. "Well, at least not the goblins. I'm pretty sure. And probably not the elves either."

She shook her head. "You cannot trust them. They only want the blade."

"The elves don't even believe that it exists. The king doesn't care about me. His daughter asked him to protect me, and he agreed."

She slumped back against her seat. "Oh, you are so very young. Don't you know that everyone involved in the game was shown the blade? The elf king saw it himself. He knows it exists, and he wants it."

Bile crept up my throat. Could it be true? Was everything Elena had told me a lie? I had to clear my throat before I could speak. "Fine, maybe I can't trust the elves. And I'm not stupid enough to ever trust Sebastian. But I can trust Mistral."

She lifted a brow. "Can you? You seem quite

different now, practically *shining* with celestial magic. Was he the one to bring it out in you?"

My pulse kicked up a notch. "What do you know about it?"

She leaned forward again. "I know that you're a celestial. And I know that these men will drain your magic dry."

"That's not true."

"Then why are you still searching, Evelyn?" Her words were clipped. "Or do you suddenly have an unquenchable thirst for power?"

I shifted uncomfortably in my seat. "Everyone only came after me because of the bounty. As long as that exists, I'll never be safe. I don't want to get my mom killed. In fact, as pissed as I am, I want to help her. I want to find whoever offered the bounty."

She pursed her lips, studying me for a moment, then she shook her head. "You'll never manage it. Take the elf king's protection for what it is, and let the rest go. Eventually they'll see that you cannot find your mother, and they'll leave you alone." She leaned forward even further, lowering her voice to a whisper. "But if you start hopping around other realms, they are all just going to want you *more*."

I tried to think of how I could explain things to her. To tell her why I couldn't let it go, especially now that I knew the extent of Mistral's problems.

But I had no good answer. Even before the bounty, I

was hell-bent on finding my mom. "Why did she take my memories?" I asked abruptly.

"For your own safety. The only reason the people after her aren't after you too is because she left you behind."

"But—"

Suddenly Gabriel was standing over us. I had been so caught up in our conversation, I hadn't been paying attention to who came and left the diner.

Marcie looked up at him. If she was intimidated by his size, she didn't show it.

Ignoring her, he looked at me. "We need to go. There are several fairies waiting outside. Gladiola overheard their intent to ambush you."

My jaw fell open.

"I told you this would happen," Marcie accused.

I glared at her. "No one else knew about this meeting. *I'm* not the one who led them here."

Her breath hissed through her clenched teeth. "I'll admit, I've drawn some unwanted attention. But it's not me they're after. It's *you*." She gave me a dark look. "You share her blood, Evelyn. Without you, only another celestial could find her. But *with* you," she stood, even with her less than impressive height managing to loom over me, "with you, they could bring her right back down to earth."

"Hence our need to depart," Gabriel growled.

Marcie sighed. "I will distract them as long as I can." She shook her head. "But it's obviously already worse than I thought. I hoped no one would figure it out." She met my eyes. "You need to hide, Evelyn. Behind a boundary where no one can reach you. But *not* with the elves."

"Wait—"

But she was already turning away.

Gabriel grabbed my arm, gently hauling me to my feet before grabbing Ringo in the messenger bag with his other hand. "The fae live beyond a boundary too. I will not let them take you where I cannot reach you."

"What did she mean? How can they use me to bring my mother down to earth?"

"I do not know. We'll figure it out once you're safe."

He tugged me toward the door, only to have the waiter block our path. He lifted his little order pad, waving it expectantly because we hadn't paid for our drinks.

One glare from Gabriel though, and he was stepping out of our path. We went for the door, stepping out into the sun. And that was when all hell broke loose.

)⁾•❂❀❂•⁽(

"THIS WAY." Gladiola intercepted us as soon as we exited the diner.

Gabriel followed her, glancing around for the fae. But they could be anywhere. Fae could easily hide in plain sight. With their glamours they could be anyone or anything. They could be—

I tugged against Gabriel's grip on my arm as Gladiola led us into an alleyway behind the diner.

Gladiola stopped ahead of us, her silver hair sweeping away from her purple tinted face as she looked back at us expectantly.

"Eva, we must—" Gabriel began.

"That's not Gladiola." I tugged back again. She looked exactly like her, but she felt wrong. I couldn't sense her goblin magic. "It's a glamour."

Gabriel cursed under his breath, shoving me behind him as Gladiola's face started to transform. In mere seconds another woman stood before us. She was smaller than Gladiola, with vibrant crimson hair. Her eyes were the same shocking red, the irises larger than a human's. Some humans liked to wear lenses to make their eyes look more fae, but this woman was the real deal.

She smiled at us, but didn't make a move, and a moment later we learned why.

Gabriel pulled me close, stepping against the wall as three more fae closed in behind us, two men and one woman, all in their true forms. They didn't all have vibrant hair like the first woman, but the eyes, the eyes would always give them away unless they changed their shape.

The first woman gave me a brilliant smile, revealing slightly pointed teeth. "Ivan sends his regards."

I inhaled sharply. I really should have tried pushing Ivan off the roof the night we rescued Braxton. "I have the protection of the elf king. Ivan would never go against Elizabeta." Or at least that's what Elena and Sebastian both thought.

"Of course not, that's why we are here." The fae closed in around us as the woman continued to speak. "We do not fear the elves. Their king stays locked away in his palace."

Gabriel had slowly maneuvered me between his back and the wall, handing me my bag with Ringo huddled inside. "You need to shift, Eva. Don't worry about me."

"I'm not leaving you." Where in the hells were the other goblins? It wasn't like we had come without backup.

"It is not me they're after."

I held onto him. I didn't need to sense magic to know the fae's dark intent. Even if I managed to shift and leave him behind, I might not see Gabriel alive again.

The crimson-haired fae drew near, her stunning eyes on Gabriel. "Leave the girl to us, and you may still be able to help the one whose face I stole." She flashed him a manic smile. "Or would you choose some half-blood celestial over one of your own people?"

My blood went cold. Gladiola. If they hurt her, it would be my fault. I had been an idiot to leave Sebastian's calling card behind.

Gabriel flexed his large hands, but he didn't move away from me. Things were about to get very ugly.

The fae woman took another step, then suddenly Gabriel was crushing me against the wall behind him. The woman cried out, and I managed to bend to one side enough to see an arrow now sticking out of her leg. My eyes followed the path the arrow would have needed to take to find Elena and two male elves standing atop of the nearest roof.

"You would dare defy a direct order of protection from the elf king?" She effortlessly hopped from the roof onto the closed lid of a dumpster, barely making a sound with her landing. She lifted her bow again, aiming it at the woman's heart. "You do know this grants me permission to kill you?"

"Stay behind me," Gabriel muttered.

As thrilled as I was to see Elena—*and* several more elves appearing on the nearest rooftops as others climbed down amongst us—I couldn't forget what Marcie had told me. The elf king knew the Realm Breaker existed and was up for grabs. His order of protection had not simply been a favor to his daughter.

In an instant, the fae all looked exactly like the elves surrounding us. All except the one who had been shot. Her face now looked like Elena, but she seemed unable to glamour the arrow sticking out of her leg.

"You can still sense their magic!" I called out to Elena.

Elena stayed on the dumpster with her bow drawn. "Is that you back there, Eva? I can hardly see you behind that massive brute." To her people, she called out, "Make sure you are close enough to sense their fairy magic before you make a kill!"

Her words made everyone move. The glamoured fae ran toward the elves, producing perfectly replicated elven blades. The clang of metal had me huddling back behind Gabriel. He started edging me along the wall toward the opening of the alley, but before we could retreat, Elena reached us.

With her back to the wall and her eyes on the fight, she spoke to me. "I have a car out front. Come with me, and we'll keep you safe in Emerald Heights."

Gabriel edged me further along. He lifted his hands as an attacker came near, then an elf darted between us, fending off the glamoured fae. "She will be coming back to the Bogs," he said through gritted teeth.

Elena snorted. "We can argue about that in the car."

We could argue, but I wasn't going back to Emerald Heights without a pretty damn good explanation. Regardless, being in a moving vehicle away from the fae sounded like an excellent idea.

We reached the corner of the diner, then slipped out of the back alley. Gabriel shoved me ahead of him to start running, but someone else was standing right there to grab me.

"How many times do I have to tell you to stop leaving your card in your apartment?" Sebastian yanked me against his chest.

A few beaten and bruised goblins staggered into the side alley behind him, Gladiola amongst them. Something tight released in my chest upon seeing her, but my relief was short-lived.

Gabriel yanked me away from Sebastian. "Your help is not needed here, devil."

Sebastian's lip lifted in a snarl. "Is this the thanks that I get for rescuing your people?"

My jaw dropped, then I realized he had probably only rescued them to figure out where I was. How he'd known to come to the diner was another problem entirely. A problem for another time.

Not appreciating being yanked around, I pulled away from Gabriel, straightened the strap of my bag, then looked at Elena. "You said something about a car?"

She flashed me a grin, then gestured toward the street. "Right this way."

Gabriel fell into step right behind me like a giant angry storm cloud. "Return to the Bogs," he said to his people as we passed them. "Tell Mistral what has happened."

The sounds of fighting were dying down behind us. I was pretty sure the elves had won—they outnumbered the fae three times over—but I wasn't going to return to find out. I would probably see something that would give me nightmares, and I had enough of those already.

"There are other fae about." Sebastian fell into step at my other side. "Be on your guard."

Despite his words, we made it out to the street unhindered. A shiny black car waited with its engine running, parked amongst all the others along the street.

I did a double take when I realized Crispin was in the driver's seat.

He rolled down the window when he saw us. "Dear Eva, how lovely to see you again!" He didn't seem put off by Gabriel and Sebastian both glaring at him in the slightest.

Elena opened the back door for me, and I had one last moment of hesitation before climbing into the car. Not because I was afraid she was going to kidnap me, not with both Gabriel and Sebastian around, but because Crispin was the one driving.

If he drove a car anything like he drove paths to other realms, we were all doomed.

14

THE CAR'S backseat felt mighty small with me sandwiched between Sebastian and Gabriel. Elena sat in the passenger seat next to Crispin, who actually seemed to be a decent driver. Although for someone driving in the city, he was really lacking in road rage. At one point someone giving him the finger had received a cheerful wave in return.

"I'm telling you, my father doesn't know about it. He would have told me." Elena was turned in her seat, straining against her seatbelt. "And who is this woman anyways? How do you know she's not lying?"

I couldn't answer that, but something told me Marcie had been telling the truth. The same thing that told me Elena was telling the truth too. Which meant her father was the liar, though I couldn't quite reconcile the idea with the kind, patient elf I had met in the palace.

Crispin stopped at a light, glancing back at me. "Not to interrupt, but we should probably decide where we're going."

"Emerald Heights," Elena said at the same time that Gabriel muttered, "The Bogs."

"Perhaps we should allow Eva to decide where she wants to go," Sebastian said pleasantly.

I angled my eyes toward him. "What exactly are you playing at?"

He gave me an innocent look.

I watched him a moment longer, but let it go. "I don't know about the rest of you, but I'm going to Willowvale."

Crispin had started to accelerate, but slammed on the brakes abruptly, making someone almost hit us. They laid on the horn, zooming around us, though he didn't seem to notice. "Willowvale? Isn't that werewolf territory?"

Elena gave me an uneasy look as Crispin eased back onto the gas. "My father would kill me if I stepped foot in Willowvale."

"The werewolves would kill you first," Gabriel muttered.

Elena eyed him sharply. "Why are you with us again?"

He glared back at her.

Sebastian seemed perfectly content to let us all argue. He'd explained that the only reason he found me was because he heard about the fairies' plan to abduct me. Being associated with the criminal underworld had its perks. Rather than warning me in the diner, he'd let me walk into an ambush. I was pretty sure it was just so he could be smug about me leaving my card behind, but he *had* helped the other goblins.

Crispin stopped at another light. "Still need to know where we're going..."

"I believe Eva already told you," Sebastian answered for me.

I narrowed my eyes at him. "Is there a reason you're okay with going to Willowvale?"

He shrugged. "Braxton and I are old friends at this point."

"No you're not. What are you up to?"

Instead of answering, he looked out the window.

"Willowvale is north, correct?" Before anyone could answer, Crispin took the next turn, heading north.

"You cannot be serious!" Elena balked.

"She doesn't want to go to Emerald Heights, Princess. And we're not in the business of kidnapping, are we?"

Elena bared her teeth at him, and I thought she might argue, then she sat back against her seat with a huff.

Ringo poked his head out of my messenger bag. "We are going to see Braxton?"

I smiled, though I still felt uneasy about whatever Braxton's mom had to say to me. "We sure are, little buddy. We sure are."

GABRIEL HAD ROLLED down his window as soon as we reached the country, and I leaned across him, inhaling the fresh air. Blades of grass swayed in rhythmic waves across rolling green hills, kissed by dappled sunlight.

I had loved coming out here with Braxton when we were teenagers, and it had been far too long since I'd been back. I had gotten too caught up with my work, and the hustle and bustle of city life.

Nothing like a few life or death experiences to really put things into perspective.

Crispin rolled down his window in front of us, letting in more greenery-scented air. "This is glorious. Why do we never come here?"

Elena slouched down in her seat with her arms crossed. "Because it's swarming with werewolves. They'll never let us through once we reach the border."

There was a chance she was right, though I didn't say so out loud. Werewolves weren't from the far realms. They didn't live behind a boundary, but they did have a *territory*. One they protected at all costs. The Willowthorn pack watched over Willowvale—aptly named after the long lineage of werewolves. I had an open invitation. Elves, goblins, and devils did not.

"Turn here," I instructed.

Crispin slowed the car, then turned right onto a narrow paved road leading up into the mountains. So far we had driven through mostly open countryside, but as we crept up the windy road, the trees started closing in around us. They had a different feel than the ones in Emerald Heights, the dark patches beneath them seeming more eerie and foreboding.

I could sense Gabriel's tension, and Elena's for that matter. While the different factions in the city had their alliances, the wolves answered to no one. Willowvale was a dangerous place to venture without invitation.

The car came to a stop as we reached a closed metal gate with a heavy padlock. Crispin glanced back at me. "What now?"

"Just wait."

It didn't take long for the wolves to appear. Two of them were in human form, and three more were full wolf, not just wolfman or wolfwoman.

Ringo scurried back into my bag as I instructed Gabriel to roll down the window the rest of the way. Crispin wisely rolled his up. The werewolves wouldn't react well if they saw a strange elf before they saw me.

I grinned as they came closer, recognizing Warrick, Braxton's cousin.

Noticing me, he met my smile with one of his own. He was just as tall as Braxton, though a little less bulky, with the same curly brown hair. Without a shirt, his deeply tanned skin was on display for all to see.

He leaned down toward the window, ignoring Gabriel. "Eva, it's about time you got out here."

"Been busy," I explained. "Did Braxton tell you I was coming?"

He nodded, finally taking a moment to observe my company. "He didn't say you'd be bringing guests though. Might be an issue."

The other werewolf in human form approached. She was tall, in her late 50s, her long black hair streaked with silver. She wore a black tank top and jeans, along with a knife at her belt, which was kind of funny considering she could sprout claws at will. Her gray eyes lingered on Gabriel, likely deeming him the greatest threat. Monica was always all business. When I was younger, I thought she didn't like me, then eventually I realized that was just how she acted toward everyone. I knew she had some scars from her past, but I had never made it my business to ask about them.

I debated my response. Would it be the worst thing to make them wait for me beyond the border? There was a small town not far. They could just go get a meal —although it was laughable picturing Gabriel, Sebastian, and the elves sitting down together for a nice late lunch.

Before I could lean one way or another, Monica shook her head. "Theresa trusts Eva." She leaned forward, making steady eye contact with me as she tilted her head. "And Eva would not bring anyone here to hurt us?" A veiled threat was evident in her tone.

"You know I wouldn't," I said evenly.

She studied me for a moment longer, then finally nodded, stepping back. "Let them through."

I didn't immediately see who she was speaking to

until another male werewolf in human form approached the padlock on the gates with a set of keys. More full wolves had edged in from the woods, watching us unblinking.

Warrick flashed me a smile. "Don't go running off too quickly. You owe me a beer."

I smiled back, though I had no intention of lingering. I might be willing to bring my strange group of companions around the wolves so I could get whatever information Braxton's mom, Theresa, had for me, but I wasn't going to leave them unattended around the werewolves. Someone would end up dead, or at least horribly injured. I was sure of it.

The gate opened, and I gave Warrick and Monica a wave as we drove through. Once Gabriel rolled up the window, everyone seemed to heave a collective sigh of relief. Well, everyone but Sebastian. He still seemed perfectly content with himself, which made me suspicious.

"This is not a good idea," Gabriel muttered as Crispin drove us further up into the mountains. "The fairies could still follow you here."

I put my hand on his arm without thinking, but a little spark of magic had me withdrawing it. Sebastian looked over at me knowingly.

I stuck my tongue out at him.

I instructed Crispin down several narrow dirt roads, knowing that Theresa would still be at work at the small local tavern. She didn't have to work—Braxton would have paid her expenses if she asked—but she liked it. It kept her social. Even amongst a tight community like the wolves, it was still possible to get cut too far adrift, like she had in the city.

She'd moved there with Braxton when he was young, wanting him to grow up with culture and opportunities. If she would have known he'd end up a mercenary, she probably would have kept him hidden away in Willowvale. It was hard to imagine how different he could have been had that occurred.

Of course, I might not even be alive right now if that had been the case. There had been no one else stepping forward to take me in after my dad died, only Theresa. I owed her my life, and so much more.

Here was hoping my visit wouldn't bring her into my mess.

Crispin parked the car next to several others in the gravel lot in front of the tavern. The tavern itself was dark wood, matching the trees all around it. The rust-colored roof seemed to absorb the sunlight rather than reflecting it.

He shut off the engine, but nobody moved.

I undid my seatbelt, moving Ringo slightly aside as he peeked back out of my bag, glancing out the window at the trees. "Okay everyone, a few ground rules. The wolves are friendly enough. We were allowed across the border, so nobody's going to question why we're here. *But* they are going to be able to smell what you are. Each and every one of you. So they're going to have *other* questions." I looked at Sebastian as I finished, "So be polite."

He gave me that innocent look again.

Shaking my head, I waited for Gabriel to open his door. This was going to be a disaster.

Gabriel climbed out, then offered me his hand, which I tentatively took. The touch felt nice, safe and warm, with only the smallest hint of magic. It wasn't so bad when emotions weren't heightened, and I could tell he was doing all he could to lock his away. Instead of looking at me, he looked toward the tavern, and the familiar werewolf walking outside.

Braxton lit up as he saw me. "It's about time!"

I released Gabriel's hand. "You do know it takes hours to get out here, and you just called me this morning."

He waved me off, then stopped short as Crispin and Elena both got out of the car. He gave Elena a nod, then looked Crispin up and down, but didn't comment. His eyes lingered longer on Gabriel, probably because of his size.

I realized with a start that they hadn't met. The only time Gabriel had come into my apartment, Ringo had given him the keys.

I introduced both Gabriel and Crispin, then as Sebastian came around the car to stand behind me, I added, "And of course, you've had the misfortune of meeting Sebastian."

Braxton rubbed his hands together, seeming a little

nervous. "You know Eva, when I told my mom you might be bringing a friend or two, I really didn't expect... *this*." His eyes flicked once more to Gabriel.

At least now I knew why Monica had actually let us in. "It's a long story. I've had an... eventful morning."

Elena snorted. "I'd call a battle to the death with fairies a little more than an *event*."

Braxton's thick brows knitted together. "Please tell me she's kidding."

"A princess *never* kids," Crispin said jokingly, then laughed. "Trust me."

"It's actually fitting if what my mom has to tell you is true." Braxton gave me a sad look. "Come on, I'll buy you a beer."

I followed him toward the entrance, letting the others line up behind me. "You know, your cousin is for some reason under the impression that I owe *him* a beer."

"You did tell him he couldn't climb to the top of that tree." Braxton held the door open for me.

"Yeah, and he couldn't. It snapped as soon as he got to the top."

Braxton laughed. "Yeah, he broke his arm, but he *did* climb to the top."

Shaking my head, I walked into the tavern and was quickly enveloped by old memories. Though we'd lived in the city, Theresa had brought us out here most weekends. I had loved coming out to the woods. After losing my father, being around so many werewolves felt oddly safe. I had no parents, and no siblings, but the werewolves treated everyone like they were family.

I looked past the rough wood tables with a few werewolves all locking their eyes on us. Theresa stood behind the bar, refilling salt shakers. Her dark eyes lit up as she saw me. "Eva!" She hurried around the bar. She was looking older now, her loose purple dress skimming a bit of extra weight, and her dark brown hair now had more gray. But she moved like a woman half her age. Hells, she moved like a teenager. One of the benefits of being a pure blooded werewolf.

She gripped my arms as she reached me, sparing a glance for my strange group of companions. Ringo wiggled out of my bag, looking boldly up at her.

"Oh!" She leaned down in front of him. "What a charming creature."

"This is Ringo." I took a moment to introduce everyone else, but she seemed more interested in the tiny goblin that had now scurried up to my shoulder to get a better look around.

She beamed at him for a moment longer, then turned knowing eyes back to me. "You feel different, Eva. What have you been up to?"

My cheeks burned as I dutifully avoided looking at any of the guys. "How much did Braxton tell you?"

She gripped my arm. "Not enough." She looked at Braxton. "Find a table and make sure our guests are comfortable. Eva is coming back to the kitchen with me." She hesitated, glancing once more at Ringo. "Can he speak?"

I nodded.

"Then perhaps he should stay behind too. What I have to say is for you alone, and you may tell who you choose, and only who you choose."

My heart fluttered in my throat. What could she possibly need to tell me? Why had Braxton dragged me out here, knowing all that was happening in my life?

Reading my expression, she patted my arm. "All will be well, Eva."

Not sure if I believed her, I lifted Ringo from my shoulder and held him out to Gabriel.

Gabriel scowled, but took the little goblin, holding him in the palms of his hands.

"He likes french fries," I said pointedly. "And cake."

Ringo sat up a little straighter, his nerves assuaged by the mention of his favorite foods, which was exactly the reaction I was going for.

"Well," Braxton said, "this is going to be interesting." He gestured for everyone to follow him as Theresa led me back past the bar.

As she opened one side of the double doors leading into the kitchen, I glanced back to see Gabriel, Sebastian, and Crispin all watching me. It was a very strange feeling, suddenly realizing how they had all become a big part of my life in a very short time. Maybe Crispin a little less, but if we got the chance to continue working together...

I cast away my thoughts, following Theresa into the kitchen.

My mouth watered at the smell of burgers on the grill, and french fries sizzling in hot oil. The steamy air made me sweat, bringing about more memories. Even after Theresa had left the city, Braxton and I would still come out here. I'd helped out in the kitchen a few times for extra cash. Then Dawn had offered me a job at the agency, and life had become very different.

Theresa glanced at the lone werewolf manning the grill, an older gentleman, six feet tall and rail thin. His name was Alfred, and he didn't speak much. But he *could* listen, so Theresa pulled me into the walk-in freezer.

I got a little nervous as she shut the door behind us, even though I knew it didn't lock. The cool air instantly gelled the sweat on my skin.

"Sorry about the chill, but it will be difficult for anyone to overhear us in here." She reached into a bag on the shelf, pulling out a handful of chocolate chips. She handed me half of them.

Smiling, I took them. She had always given me chocolate when I was younger too.

When her expression turned suddenly serious, my hand clamped around the cold little chips. "Eva, I have something to tell you, and I hope you won't be upset with me. Your father made me promise to keep it to myself unless at some point I deemed it necessary for you to know."

My gut clenched with sudden dread at her tone. My breath whooshed out of me, fogging the air around my face.

"I don't know how to say this," she continued, "so I will just spill it quickly." It seemed to take her some effort to meet my eyes. "When your father got sick, when he realized he wasn't going to make it, he told me a secret. He told me why your mother left."

Blood rushed in my ears, and against the cold air, I felt faint. "He said he didn't know."

She reached for my arm, but I pulled away, and her face fell. "Eva, it was far too dangerous for you. He did not support her in taking your memories, and he felt quite sure she'd taken some of his as well, but there was one thing he remembered."

I stared at her, my heart in my throat, waiting for the other shoe to drop.

"Your mother had lived a long time before she had you," she reluctantly continued. "And your father learned—" She met my eyes. "Your father learned that she was the one who severed the paths to the other realms, and powerful people wanted her dead because of it."

15

I STORMED out of the walk-in, the heat right outside the door feeling suffocating. Or maybe it was just the emotions that swam within me. He knew why she left. He knew why she abandoned me, and he had let me think that she didn't want me.

Theresa hurried out after me. "You must understand, Eva. It was for your own protection. Anything you knew could put you in danger."

I spun on her, tears stinging my eyes. "I have been looking for her for *years*. I have been looking for her most of my life."

She glanced at the grill, but Alfred was nowhere to be seen. Maybe he'd sensed us coming. "There's more you need to know."

"More?" I choked out. "How could there be more?"

She grabbed my arm, pulling me back toward the

walk-in, but not inside it. She tugged me close, then lowered her voice. "Not long after your mom left, someone came looking for her. I think she had hoped that no one knew about you and your father. She left as soon as she thought someone might find her, but she left too late. The woman who came was clearly a celestial. Your father was human, but he said he could tell. When he told her your mother was gone, she asked about you."

My emotions thrummed through me like electricity. I wanted to pull away, to go back to the city, but I remained rooted to the spot.

"He didn't know what she wanted with you, but he feared she might try to take you. So he went to the fairies."

My eyes flew wide. "What could he have wanted with them?"

She sighed heavily. "You know of their glamours."

I did know of their glamours. I had seen them just a few hours ago, but—

"He made a trade with them. He asked them to fake your death." She squeezed my arm. "Eva, I don't know if your mother ever came back for you, but she wouldn't have found you, because to her, and *only* to her, you look like someone else."

"That's why he changed our names," I breathed.

She nodded, her face creased with sympathetic lines. "You look different to her, but someone living under her daughter's name would have drawn her interest, and she would have figured it out. But your father covered everything. Your mother thinks you're dead. It was the only way he could think to protect you. To make it like you no longer existed, so no one else would come looking."

I inhaled sharply, refusing to let my tears fall. "She no longer thinks I'm dead," I said evenly. "*Everyone* knows I'm her daughter."

But had she really destroyed the paths to the other realms? Was it even possible? Sebastian had claimed that she was old, but I just couldn't quite reconcile the story in my mind with the previous idea I'd had of my mother. And of my father.

Theresa watched me, probably waiting for me to break down, or to at least react.

But I suddenly felt entirely empty. "Why are you telling me this now? Why after all of these years?"

"Braxton told me what happened. He told me about the bounty on your mother, and about bad people being after you. I thought you needed to know everything." She squeezed my arm. "I only wanted to keep you safe, Eva. And that's what your father wanted too."

I pulled out of her grip. I knew her words were true. I knew I shouldn't be mad at her. But I had also been lied to my entire life. "I just need a moment to myself." I abruptly walked away from her, back out into the tavern, then quickly skirted the growing crowd and headed for the bathroom.

I locked the door behind me, then unclenched my shaking hands. In one palm the chocolate chips had melted into a brown sticky mess. I turned on the faucet, rubbing my hands vigorously beneath the cold stream of water, until finally I lifted my gaze to the mirror, meeting my eyes in my reflection.

It was a mistake. I wasn't sure who the person was standing there. Did I even look like myself? Or was it a glamour?

No, Theresa had claimed the glamour was aimed at my mother. I would only look different to her, not to myself. And that was how Sebastian had originally recognized me, because in reality, I looked a lot like my mom.

I dried my hands with a paper towel, then pushed my hair back out of my face before dabbing at the few tears that had escaped my eyes.

Nothing was different, not really. Just now I knew that my dad had lied to me, and that my mother really had thought I was dead. When she tasked Lucas with killing night runners, she didn't realize I would be at risk.

Of course, that didn't change the fact that she was willing to kill innocent people to keep herself safe. Something like that simply wasn't forgivable.

So why was I still protecting her?

I straightened my hair and clothing as much as possible, but there was nothing I could do about the red rims around my eyes. I left the bathroom, then headed for the table where everyone waited.

Sebastian was the first to notice me, and as he turned to watch my approach, I couldn't quite read his strange expression.

Braxton noticed me next, and he watched me warily, comprehending the news I had just received.

As the others turned toward me, their expressions were a mixture of hope, curiosity, and the same wariness. Everyone but Braxton was depending on me, in very different, but also in some ways similar, regards. They had all gotten drinks. A beer for Braxton, what looked like hot green tea for Elena and Crispin, water for Gabriel, and black coffee for Sebastian. There were a few menus strewn about, but no food.

"Mom came out to take our orders," Braxton said evenly, like he was speaking to a spooked horse. "I figured you'd be alright with a burger."

I nodded, then slumped into the vacant seat beside him with Sebastian to my left. Gabriel had made the valiant sacrifice of sitting at the devil's other side, with Ringo perched on the edge of the table beside him.

I looked across the table at Elena and Crispin. "Sorry for dragging you both out here. Once we eat, if you don't mind dropping the rest of us off in the city, you can get back to Emerald Heights."

Elena tried to act casual, but her green eyes were pinched with worry. "That werewolf woman told you something you didn't like."

I frowned. I was among friends... kind of. But that

didn't mean I was about to spill my guts. "I've learned a lot of things lately that I'm not terribly fond of. It's nothing important to anyone else though."

Except maybe Mistral. He had given my mom a place to hide before she left the realm. He claimed he didn't know what she was hiding from, and it was a good thing. If she really destroyed the paths to other realms—

I cut off my own thoughts, reaching for Braxton's beer.

"Hey!" One look at my expression and he stopped his protests, lifting his hands. "I guess I'll be going to get another beer." He pushed out his seat, then walked toward the bar.

Crispin lifted his white mug of tea. "Well I for one don't mind this little side adventure. *Most* of us have never had the opportunity to enter werewolf lands."

"They're just like any other woods," Elena scoffed. "Not like something behind a boundary."

He leaned his shoulder near hers. "But it's the *culture* dear princess. Look around you." Mug in one hand, he swept the other around him, gesturing to the werewolves who had quickly gone back to minding their own business. "It's fascinating. No magic necessary. They were *born* to watch over this land."

"Keep your voice down," Elena hissed when a particularly burly werewolf glanced back from the bar at Crispin's words.

Crispin pouted. "But I was being *complementary*."

When Gabriel finally deigned to speak, it was to say, "No boundary means no protection from the fairies."

My gut squirmed at the mention of the fae. They were as long-lived as elves, maybe even longer. Some claimed they were truly immortal. That meant that whichever fairy my dad had made a bargain with, they were likely still alive. If I could find them, I could ask them the truth of what occurred.

Elena tsked. "Those *particular* fairies won't be harming anyone else." She inhaled deeply. "But yes, their people may be an issue going forward. We can only hope that they are simply working for Ivan, and have no interest in the bounty themselves. Once we deal with Ivan, they may go away."

Braxton returned to the table, holding multiple bottles by their necks. He set one in front of each of us, then gave everyone a dark look. "Apparently our pack alpha welcomes you all to our lands. I would advise against refusing his offerings." He gestured to the beers.

My eyes widened, but Sebastian chose that moment to lean in near my shoulder. "A word?"

Gabriel's eyes darted toward us, but I shook my head. I appreciated his protection, but I didn't need it from Sebastian. At least not yet. "We can go outside."

He stood, offering me his hand, which I ignored. I stood and walked past him toward the door, and soon we were out in the fresh air, beyond the parking lot standing amongst the trees.

I felt a surge of his magic, then opened my mouth wide enough for my ears to pop. I realized he was probably protecting us from any eavesdroppers, just as he had done before at the café when he'd first offered me a job.

He turned toward me. "Learning that your mother may have destroyed the paths to the other realms is a good step in our search. It narrows down the people who would want her dead."

My jaw dropped. "Were you spying on me?"

He gave me a tired look.

"You asshole!" I balled my fists. "Theresa said what she had to say in private for a reason."

"Just as I eavesdropped on your conversation for a *reason*. And now we must consider a rather blatant contradiction."

Still fuming, I grumbled, "Oh yeah? And what is that?"

He sighed. "Sometimes I give you far too much credit. If your mother really destroyed the paths to the far realms, she would have needed the Realm Breaker to do it. And yet, it is being offered as a reward for her deliverance. So she had it back then, but not now. Now, we just need to figure out who could have taken it from her."

I blinked at him. He was right. If he'd seen the blade

himself, presented to him from behind a strong shield of glamour by the person offering the bounty, then my mother no longer had it. The sword's power would be unmistakable to someone like Sebastian. If he thought it was the real deal, then I believed him.

But just how had my mother come across it to begin with? And why would she have destroyed the pathways?

"I see you understand. I believe our first step should be figuring out at what point she lost the blade. And I think you know exactly who to ask." He lowered his chin and lifted his brows.

I glared at him. "If she had the blade when Mistral helped her leave the realm, I'm sure he would have noticed."

"Perhaps he did, and he simply neglected to tell you."

I started to shake my head, then stopped. It was a possibility that he had chosen just the right words to avoid a lie, but I didn't think so. He'd said he didn't know why she was running. If she had the blade, he would've known exactly why. Of course knowing something for a *fact* and thinking it only a possibility were two very different things. So he could have said he didn't *know* why she was running without breaking our bargain.

But I really didn't think that was the case. Not now. "I'll ask him, but I'm pretty sure she lost the blade before that point. And it's been a *long* time since the pathways were destroyed. She could have lost it at any point before then."

"Then the question is, who would have not only had the means to procure the blade, but the motivation to punish her for using it? For this person to have hunted her for so long, it is clearly personal. My first guess would be a family member." Harsh light cut across his face as the sun began to set.

"You think her own flesh and blood has hunted her for years, forcing her to abandon her husband and daughter?"

He shrugged. "It is not such an unusual concept. A mere rival would have given up long ago. As I said, this is personal. What did you learn from the celestial woman this morning?"

"You mean you weren't *spying* then?"

He wrinkled his nose. "I learned of the fae plot shortly before my arrival to thwart them."

I smiled. "Ooh, I like having something you don't know."

His eyes darkened. "Do not play games, Eva."

"Why not? You always do." Grinning, I turned and sauntered back toward the tavern, brushing against his dark magic as I exited the bubble of privacy he had afforded us.

Normally Braxton was the one to cheer me up, but messing with Sebastian did the job quite nicely. I still had a sick feeling in my stomach, but I needed to move forward. After so many years of searching, I was finally getting answers. That's what was important. At the end of our road, was the truth.

And I would continue barreling toward it, letting the chips fall where they may.

16

I walked back into the tavern to find the alpha of the Willowthorn pack had taken my empty seat. The food had arrived, along with another round of beers.

I stayed just inside the doorway for a moment, fighting a grin as I watched Elena squirming in her seat. She probably had no idea what to expect from the alpha werewolf, and I had a feeling he was taking advantage of that.

Quite the prankster, was old Harry.

Sebastian appeared just behind me. "Now that you've learned all you can, we should go."

"No more pressuring me about the oh so secret information that I have and you don't?"

He sighed heavily. "I imagine you won't be able to keep it to yourself for long."

I laughed. "We'll see, but either way, we can't go yet. The local alpha has welcomed us to his table.

Gabriel might be willing to be rude, but I imagine Elena will try to observe protocol."

He moved to my side, observing the stout man seated at our table. His curly, gray streaked brown hair was unkempt, falling past his shoulders, though not quite as long as his beard. He wore a blue T-shirt, something with a logo on the front, though from the angle I couldn't see what it said. Torn jeans completed the look. With his big hands and sun-chapped skin, he would have fit in at any construction site.

"*That* is the local alpha?"

I gave Sebastian a sidelong glance. "So many things you don't seem to know tonight. I must say, you have considerably brightened my mood." I walked away from him toward the table.

"Eva!" Harry stood as he saw me, wrapping me in a big bear hug, lifting my feet off the floor.

I hugged him back for a moment, then patted his arm. "Can't quite breathe, Harry."

He let me down abruptly, giving me an abashed smile. "Sorry girl, you know I always forget you're not actually a wolf."

"A high compliment, coming from you." I took what had been Sebastian's seat, gesturing for Harry to keep mine.

Braxton was grinning from ear to ear, and Elena's cheeks were bright red. Ringo's face was buried so deep into a little plastic basket of french fries that he barely acknowledged me returning to the table.

Braxton slid another basket with a burger and fries on parchment paper toward me, waggling his eyebrows at me. We were on his turf now, where he felt most comfortable. I always loved seeing him like this.

I smiled in return, and any lingering tension around his eyes dissipated. Yeah, I was hurt and confused by what Theresa had told me, but now that I'd had time to recover, it wasn't the end of the world. In fact, I was beginning to suspect that maybe my mom wasn't the bad guy. At least not completely. She hadn't left because she didn't want me. She had left because she was being chased. Mistral had suggested it, and now Theresa had confirmed it.

I lifted a fry as Harry sat. "Your elf friends were just telling me about your time in Emerald Heights."

I stiffened. They wouldn't tell him...

"I would have killed to see you riding that buck," he continued with a laugh. "I remember that summer my tia tried to take you horseback riding."

The mention of horses had me glancing at Gabriel. "I'm a little more comfortable on horses now than I used to be."

Gabriel offered me a small smile, though I could tell something was wrong. He was even more broody than usual. If I had to guess, he was worried about Mistral. He should have been in the Bogs protecting his prince, instead he was out here protecting me. At least Gladiola would have told Mistral by now what had happened.

I held his gaze for a moment longer, then nodded

toward the vacant pool table at the other side of the room. "I'll be right back, Harry. If you want a real story, you should ask Elena about the time she went undercover at a vampire bar."

Elena's cheeks burned even brighter.

I gave her a teasing grin, then snatched a few more fries as I pushed away from the table. Not muttering a word to the others, Gabriel followed me. I noticed Sebastian at the bar as we retreated, being handed a glass of red wine. Rolling my eyes, I kept walking.

Gabriel and I ended up in a darkened corner near the pool table. I fiddled with a cue stick, though I had no intention of actually playing. "If you need to get back to the Bogs, I could see about finding you a car to borrow."

"I don't drive," his voice rumbled lowly from within his chest.

I lifted my brows, though I supposed it made sense. With Mistral unable to leave the Bogs, I doubted Gabriel left much either. "There is no way Harry is letting me leave so soon, but maybe Crispin can drive you, and I can find a car to drive the rest of us..."

His dark eyes finally met mine. "I'm not leaving you. Especially not with Elena."

"You don't think—"

His gaze slid across the room, watching her nervously sipping her beer. "How did she know where to find you? You did not tell her about your meeting at the diner."

"Maybe she got the same intel that Sebastian did."

"Convenient."

I moved closer to him, not wanting to risk being overheard by the werewolves in the room. *Or Sebastian.* He had returned to the table with his wine, but that didn't mean he wasn't somehow listening in. Oh well. I turned my back on everyone, then stood on tiptoe to reach Gabriel's ear, bracing myself with a hand against his chest, careful not to touch bare skin. "I think I believe her. Even if her father actually saw the Realm Breaker, I don't think he told her."

I felt him tense beneath my palm. "That does not mean that he has no ulterior motives for offering you his protection. He may have sent her to the diner."

"Maybe," I agreed. "Either way, there's nothing we can do about it tonight."

I was close enough that I couldn't see his face, but I imagined he would be glowering. "I'm not leaving you alone with them."

"Fine, but that means you're not going to make it back to the Bogs any time soon. Harry is a friendly guy, but he's still alpha. You don't enter werewolf lands, then refuse the alpha's hospitality."

"What did Sebastian have to say to you?"

My breath went out of me. Maybe I was recovering from the news, but thinking of everything still made me dizzy. "He was spying on my conversation with Theresa. He heard everything."

Gabriel went extremely still. I knew he wanted to know what I had learned, but I also knew he wouldn't push me for the information. He would let me tell him if, or when I wanted to. "It's a long story, and I don't want anyone else to hear. We'll discuss it with Mistral once we're back in the Bogs."

He moved his head slightly, brushing his cheek against mine. Just the small touch made me shiver, made my breath catch in my throat. We still hadn't discussed our kiss, hadn't discussed the tension between us. Hadn't discussed the possibility of exploring my magic further.

I remained close to him as the first sparks of magic ignited between us.

"Eva—"

"I know," I breathed, pulling away enough to meet his eyes. I tried to convey what I was thinking. That I didn't think the kiss was a mistake. But I didn't want to say it out loud where Sebastian might hear. *Some* things were actually supposed to be private.

As if he could actually tell what I was thinking, he nodded, but I could tell he still wanted to say something.

"What is it?" I asked.

"The celestial woman, she called you Evelyn."

My shoulders tensed, then I forced them to relax. "That was my name. Evelyn Waters. When mom left my dad changed our surname to Nixey, a name from way back in his family line, and I started going by Eva."

"Eva Nix," he said.

I nodded. "I shortened it when I was older. I thought it had a nice ring to it."

He smiled, and it was such a rare, warm expression from him that I smiled too.

"Thank you for telling me."

I squeezed his arm, then stepped away from him just as Warrick sauntered into the tavern with two of his friends. He spotted me almost immediately, diverging from his two friends as they headed toward the bar.

He threw an arm around me, swarming my senses with werewolf power and the slight smell of wet dog. "How about that beer?"

"I don't owe you any beers. The tree *broke*." I looked back, giving Gabriel an apologetic smile before allowing Warrick to lead me toward the bar.

"The bet was that I could make it to the top. I did."

I laughed. "Fine. One beer." I really shouldn't be spending the money since I hadn't been taking on any new jobs, but I was also starting to think I could fire some of my private investigators. I was pretty sure at this point that if anyone was going to find my mom, it was going to be me.

"That's my girl."

Spotting us, Crispin hopped up from the table, meeting us at the bar. "I offered to buy the next round," he told us with a grin. "Am I an expert at werewolf culture, or what?"

Warrick lifted a brow. "Don't get out very often?"

Crispin shrugged. "Well I only came to this realm

fifty some odd years ago, and much of that time has been consumed by my research. You see, werewolves are not native to my realm."

"Oookay," I cut him off. "Enough realm talk. Do you even have any money?"

He held up a credit card slipped between two of his fingers. "It pays to escort a princess."

Warrick finally removed his arm from around me, but it was only so he could face both of us. "What's this about a princess?"

An evil idea crossed my mind. "An *elf* princess," I emphasized. "She's right over there."

"You're a good friend, Eva." Warrick clapped me on the arm. "Consider your debt repaid." He turned away from the bar, heading straight for the table.

A smile slowly formed on Crispin's lips. "My, you're a bit wicked, aren't you?"

I laughed. "He's harmless, and it will be fun to see just how red Elena's cheeks can get."

He ordered the next round of drinks, then turned back to me. "I think you're the perfect friend for her. She deserves to have some fun."

I rolled my eyes toward him. "It seems like *you'd* be the perfect friend for her. Do you ever take anything seriously?"

He shrugged. "Some things."

"How did you know to find me at the diner?"

He seemed taken aback. "You mean you don't know?"

I waited expectantly.

"You have the protection of our king, Eva. How would it look to have you killed out somewhere in the city?"

My jaw fell open. That meant— "You mean he had me followed?"

"Of course. As soon as our sentries noticed the fairies following you, Elena and I came right away." He rolled his eyes. "Oh don't look at me like that. You can't be perfectly fine with goblins following you around, only to scoff when elves do it too."

I shut my mouth. Everyone at the table would be wanting their drinks, but... Had the king really spared so many people to protect me, just because his daughter asked him? Or was there more to it? "Does Elena really believe her father knows nothing about the...mythical object?" Crispin's expression sobered considerably. "I've been wondering about that, actually. Elena was the first to bring news of the bounty, but when she told her father, he told her the blade did not exist. It was all some sort of scam."

My brows lifted. "You heard him say that?"

He nodded. "At first I thought little of it, and believed he must be right. As far as I was aware previously, the blade was indeed a myth."

We both turned as the bartender set several open bottles on the bar. Crispin gave her his card—or was it Elena's card?—and told her to keep the tab open.

I met the bartenders eyes, but it didn't seem like

she'd heard anything we were saying. The noise had picked up considerably in the tavern, but we still needed to be careful.

I sidled closer, lowering my voice. "And what do you believe now?"

A hint of worry flashed in his eyes, then was gone. "I believe Elena needs to speak with her father."

17

IT WAS two in the morning by the time we managed to escape the tavern. Harry had been in fine form, jumping in with one of his own stories as soon as someone else finished. It had gone on for ages, leaving Elena drunk, Gabriel cranky, Crispin with tired bags under his eyes and Sebastian... well he was still as oddly cheerful as ever. Ringo had fallen asleep in my bag around 10 PM, and hadn't stirred since, not even when we moved to the car and started our way back down the mountain.

I had left Braxton with a promise to call him once I made it somewhere safe, which hopefully wouldn't be an issue as long as we didn't run into any more Fae. Gabriel and I would go to the Bogs first to make sure everything was alright with Mistral, then as soon as Elena procured another charm for Sebastian, he and I would return to Emerald Heights.

I didn't like bringing a devil bodyguard, but I'd had far too many close calls. If I didn't learn to exercise a little caution, I was going to end up dead. Or trapped in the Crystal Vale. Humans stayed away from the fae realm within the city, and I was with them. Most who managed to cross the boundary never returned.

But my father. Had he really gone there? And what could he have offered the fae to fake my death?

"What an unbearably long drive," Elena sighed dramatically from the front seat.

I wasn't sure how many beers she'd had, I knew at least six. "We haven't even made it to the border yet."

"Uuughhh."

I chuckled, looking over at Gabriel, noting the strong bridge of his nose over the grim line of his mouth. A wave of guilt made my throat tight. Mistral had seemed fine with lending him to me. After we put the vines back in their place, he had made it seem like it wasn't likely to happen again soon. But then why was Gabriel so worried?

"There's something happening up ahead." Crispin's words cut through my thoughts. He'd had only had two beers, along with a large meal, so he was fine to drive, and sounded more alert than ever.

Wrapping my arms around my bag containing Ringo, I leaned forward in my seat, peering out the dark windshield.

But it was too cloudy, leaving us in almost pitch

blackness beyond the range of the headlights. "I don't see anything."

"Elves see better than most anyone," Elena said proudly, then giggled.

"She is correct," Crispin agreed, "so you're just going to have to trust me. There's movement up ahead, near the border." He slowed the car. "Perhaps we should take a moment to scout the road. This could be a trap."

It was odd hearing Crispin sound so serious and capable, so far from his normally affable demeanor.

Gabriel pressed against my side, peering out the windshield. "If the fae managed to track us, they would have had trouble at the border."

His words were like an injection of ice into my veins. If we had led the fae here... The werewolves were capable of protecting their lands, but there would be casualties. And those casualties would be completely my fault.

"No slowing down. If something happens they may need our help." I looked at Sebastian, relaxed in his seat. "*All* of our help."

He lifted a brow. "You expect me to protect were-wolves now?"

"Yes. I do."

I didn't have time to see if he agreed. Our headlights bounced across the bare metal of the twisted gate at the border, and I suddenly was able to see the *movement*

Crispin had spotted. It was difficult to tell in the blaring headlights if they were fae, but considering that they were fighting with werewolves to enter their lands, it seemed likely. A few figures waited on motorcycles beyond the ruined gates, revving their engines in preparation to charge through while others fought werewolves in both human and wolf form all around.

"Fae," Crispin confirmed, hitting the brakes.

"Shit. What do we do?" Gods, this was my fault. I was glad Theresa and Braxton were still back at the tavern, but Monica could be out there in danger, along with countless other wolves who had nothing to do with my mom or any of this horrible mess.

A giant wolf tumbled into the street in front of us with a small fae woman gripping its fur. With her inhuman strength, she smacked the wolf's head against the road.

There was no time to wait for an answer. Gabriel was already reaching for the door, but anyone who got out was as good as dead. I gripped his arm. "No, just roll down the windows." I looked at Crispin in the rearview mirror. "You're going to have to hit the gas. Try not to run over any wolves."

His features tight, he answered me with a single nod. Gabriel still hadn't rolled down the window. The Fae had noticed us now. The wolf right in front of us launched the woman from its body, then it got up and ran. The woman quickly righted herself, grinning at us through the windshield. The motorcycle engines revved.

"Okay go!" I reached around Gabriel and pushed the button to lower the window as the car lurched forward.

"You're too late, assholes!" I yelled out the window, getting everyone's attention. "If you want to catch me you better keep up!"

Realizing our intent, the fae on motorcycles sped toward the side of the road, then looped around in the dirt, immediately giving chase the moment we passed.

"So nice of you to ensure they follow us," Sebastian said tersely beside me over the sound of shouts and roaring engines.

"Better than leaving them to kill the wolves." I clung to Gabriel's arm, looking behind us as the car barreled down the dark road.

Seven lights followed us, so at least seven fae, maybe more if some rode two to a bike, which I had spotted a few. I knew Sebastian could hold his own in a fight, and Gabriel probably could too, though he had no weapon. Elena had put her bow in the trunk, and probably could barely aim right now despite her sitting stiffly in her seat, knocked right back into relative soberness.

Gabriel watched the pursuing fae. "They'll try to run us off the road before we can reach the city."

"I'll try to avoid that." Crispin gripped the steering wheel tight enough to make his knuckles go white. If we could make it to the highway, we might be all right, but the twisting mountain roads were perilous at such high speeds. If anything appeared ahead of us, we were cooked.

"Stop!"

Crispin saw what Elena was shouting about a moment later and slammed on the brakes, skidding toward a massive pine tree that had been freshly felled across the road. I was grateful for my seatbelt as my body was thrown forward. Sebastian's hand darted in front of me, grabbing the messenger bag with Ringo inside before he could get flung into the windshield.

My blood rushed in my ears, and I could hear nothing over my pounding heart. Then I heard the motorcycle engines, and shouting all around.

Gabriel flung away his seatbelt, leaning in front of me to look at Sebastian. "Can you get her out of here?"

"I cannot travel with anyone else," Sebastian calmly replied, handing me the bag with Ringo.

The poor little goblin trembled against me, and that was my fault too. I had brought him into this.

Crispin looked back at us. "But Eva can shift. If she's gone, perhaps the rest of us can escape on foot."

"Make your choices quickly," Sebastian said. "I can only hold them off for so long." He disappeared in a flash of black.

A moment later, one of the approaching fae screamed.

"Holy hells," Crispin muttered. He looked at me.

"You need to realm jump, Eva. You're the one they want."

My breath heaved out of me. He was right. They wanted me. They would *follow* me. I shoved Ringo into Gabriel's lap, then scooted into Sebastian's seat, going for the door.

"Eva," Gabriel growled. I shifted just slightly, evading his grip, then I was out in the night.

A male fairy with vibrant orange hair gelled into spikes reached for me almost instantly. I shifted enough to avoid his grip, then Sebastian was there in a flash of black. I didn't see a blade, but suddenly the fairy was clutching his neck, blood turned black by the moonlight welling between his fingers.

"Run," Sebastian hissed into my ear.

He didn't have to tell me twice. I ran toward the woods, both dreading that they would follow me, and hoping they would. If I could lead enough of them away, Sebastian could deal with the rest.

I didn't make it far before someone else grabbed for me, then Gabriel was there, flinging a full grown fae male aside like he weighed nothing. "Go!" Gabriel grunted.

My sneakers struggled to gain traction on damp grass as I threw myself forward, sprinting toward the trees. I focused on shifting, just enough to make me difficult to grab. I wasn't about to leave the guys completely behind, even if I could figure out how to realm jump with just a thought.

I sensed my pursuers more than I heard them. Someone was close, right at my heels. Then the earth erupted below me and I toppled head over heels. I landed hard against a tree trunk, sucking in a painful breath as I looked at the space where I'd been. A screaming female was wrapped entirely in unearthed tree roots, being crushed by their sinewy lengths.

For a moment I was stunned, remembering the vines from the Bogs, then I remembered that Crispin was technically a wizard. His magic was weaker in this realm, but not gone entirely.

I saw two more figures heading my way, neither tall enough to be one of the guys, and definitely not the right shape for Elena. I sucked in another heavy breath, got to my feet, and kept running.

Two I could deal with. Sebastian had eliminated at least one, and so had Crispin and Gabriel. If I could lead these two away, hopefully they could take care of the rest. The fairies probably hadn't bargained on facing a devil, an elven wizard, and a goblin that looked like he could probably bench press a car. At least not all at once.

I wove through the trees growing denser around me, my lungs burning with exertion. My thighs were already beginning to feel like jelly. I dared a glance back, but I didn't see either of my pursuers. Then I turned around too late. I slammed right into a stranger's arms, and he locked them tightly around me. I tried to scream, but a hand clamped over my mouth.

Shift, I had to shift. I pictured Gabriel, then Sebastian, then Crispin and Elena, but my panic quickly drowned out each image. The man who had grabbed me lifted me off my feet, then hauled me deeper into the woods.

18

I FOUGHT, kicking and screaming as the man dragged me deeper into the dark woods. I vaguely sensed a strange shift as we stepped over what felt like a boundary, then he threw me onto the ground.

Fierce pale eyes looked down at me. His hair was some other pale color, difficult to tell in the moonlight. It fell neatly to his chin, framing a sharp jaw. His clothing was black, blending into the night around us. He was fae, but he didn't seem like the others, throwing himself wildly into the chase.

No, he had calculated things perfectly. And I had run right into his waiting arms.

I realized with a start that I could no longer hear the distant fighting. Whatever strange boundary we had crossed, it blocked out all sound. I couldn't see anything beyond the surrounding trees.

"I hope Ivan is paying you well," I spat. "Because the rest of your people will soon be dead."

He sneered. "I do not work for Ivan. I do not want the blade." As if to emphasize his words, he drew a blade of his own. It was as long as his forearm, and glinted wickedly in the scant moonlight.

I started crab-crawling away, but he knelt almost too fast for my eyes to follow, grabbing onto my hair. He tugged my head to one side, bending my neck at a painful angle. Thorns and slick grass sliced across my hands as I tried to lift my neck away from the blade.

"If you kill me you'll never find my mother."

"I am saving your mother," he hissed into my ear. "Your foolishness is going to get her killed."

I went perfectly still. "*What?*" I winced as he pressed his blade against my throat. My heart hammered so forcefully I thought I might faint.

"So many fools believe your mother condemned us. They don't realize she *saved* us. And I will not let that sacrifice be in vain, even if it means the death of her progeny."

Oh gods, I'd had a lot of close calls lately, but I knew this one was it. I knew I was going to die. I closed my eyes, trying to shift, but absolutely nothing happened. It was like I had been cut off from my magic entirely. Whatever barrier he had carried me across had nullified *everything*.

Tears leaked down my face from my closed eyes. "I don't understand."

"I know you do not, and for that I am sorry. But the pathways must not be reopened. It would spell utter disaster for us all." His final words were barely a whisper. The blade pressed into my throat, drawing blood.

Even with my eyes closed, I could tell when everything went dark. So dark that not a shred of light came through. For a moment, I thought it had already happened. I thought I was already dead.

Then I felt the knife fall away from my throat. The grip on my hair loosened, and the man's body fell heavily to the earth.

I screamed when someone touched me, my renewed panic making me realize my magic was back. I pictured the guys again, preparing to shift, then someone lifted me up and a familiar voice sounded in my ear. "The idea was for you to realm jump *before* they caught you, not after your rescue."

My breath whooshed out of me. I blinked my eyes, but everything was still so dark. Then the darkness cleared. It was Sebastian carrying me in his arms. It has been *his* darkness that surrounded us.

And the one who caught me... I had no desire to look back as Sebastian carried me away. "Is he dead?"

"Yes. I had not expected a full silence charm, else I would have reached you sooner."

My heart was still racing. I couldn't seem to make it stop. And yet, despite all of the blood flow, my body felt cold. "What in the hells is a silence charm?"

"A charm to cut off not only noise and sight, but

magic. He neutralized you, knowing you might be able to escape. What did he say to you?"

As my heart finally slowed, my body started trembling. "He... He wanted to kill me to protect my mother. He said the pathways shouldn't be reopened. That it would mean disaster for us all."

"I truly hadn't expected anyone else to try to kill you, not after Lucas was set straight."

I met his eyes as he looked down at me, and my chest constricted. There was no hint of fire in his eyes, only darkness. And his dark magic still surrounded us.

"You saved me."

"Obviously."

Still looking down at me, he hoisted me up more securely, and I looped my arms around his neck. The tension between us was so taut, it felt like it could snap at any moment. I was breathing so shallowly, I felt lightheaded.

He smirked, then lifted his eyes to continue walking, breaking the tension between us in an instant.

We reached the clearing beyond the forest. I could see the car still parked in the middle of the road, headlights illuminating the fallen tree. I saw Elena kneeling on the ground, and Crispin standing over her, their eyes on something else.

"Where is Gabriel?"

"He fell to a fairy blade. I believe some manner of poison was involved. I could not wait around to learn more, considering you required my immediate attention."

A spike of ice stabbed through my chest. Gabriel, he... I fought against Sebastian until he let me down. Though my legs were still trembling, they carried me across the grass. One moment I had my eyes on Elena and Crispin, then I was standing right beside them. Ringo was there too, his little blue paws on one of Gabriel's limp hands.

Elena gasped at my sudden appearance, then her expression fell. "Eva, I'm—"

"Move." I sank to my knees, looking down at Gabriel. He lay on his back, unmoving. Elena had been holding Crispin's shirt over the wound, for what good it would do.

I reapplied pressure, then reached my other hand toward his neck, feeling for a pulse.

My heart screamed as I waited. He couldn't die because of me. He couldn't die *period*.

Relief washed through me as I felt his heart beat, but just barely. And his pulse was far too slow.

"He does not have long," Crispin said softly.

"Like hell he doesn't," I cried. I didn't know what I was doing. All I knew was that he couldn't die here in this field. All I knew was that if anyone could help, it was Mistral.

And so I clung to Gabriel, and I thought of Mistral. I thought of the Bogs, a place that was oddly starting to feel like home.

I hung my head and I cried as stars exploded all around us.

)))◑◐●◑◐(((

"Eva," Mistral said at my back. "What happened?"

I opened my eyes, looking down at Gabriel. His skin was sallow, almost gray in the moonlight. I gasped, inhaling the balmy air of the Bogs. It had worked. We had made it.

And Gabriel was still dying.

"A poisoned fairy blade, I think." I couldn't even remember who had told me that. The entire event seemed like a blur.

Mistral knelt beside me, bringing with him the scent of rain and warm vanilla. The scent relaxed me. He was here, with us. If anyone would know what to do, it was Mistral.

With nimble fingers he pulled the bloody shirt away from the wound, lifting Gabriel's tattered shirt further to give himself a clear view. There was enough moonlight for me to see the wound's jagged edges. At first I thought it was more blood, then I realized the edges had turned black.

I glanced around us, desperate to find something, *anything* to help. But I didn't recognize this place. We knelt in green grass, and around us were aspen trees, their leaves quaking in the invisible breeze.

"This is where my mother is buried," Mistral said, shocking me. "Beyond the trees over there." He nodded in that direction, then turned his gaze back down to Gabriel. "It is definitely poison, though not one I recognize. It is likely laced with magic rather than actual toxins, knowing the fae."

My throat felt so tight it was difficult to speak. "How do we help him?"

"He is a goblin, and he is now in his lands. Either the magic of our people will help him, or it will not."

I gripped his arm. "That's not good enough."

"That is all we have."

A cold feeling trickled down my spine like icy water. It wasn't good enough. We both knew it. Gabriel was going to die.

"We have to do something."

Mistral looked at me, showing me the full weight of the pain in his eyes. Gabriel was his closest friend—I had no idea how long they had been together, but I sensed it was a *very* long time.

"We *have* to do something," I repeated. "If it is the land that must heal him, then we will *make* it heal him. We controlled it before."

"It doesn't work like that, Eva."

He was probably right. He surely knew much more about it than anyone else. But... I had felt it. When we controlled the vines, I had felt his connection to the land. And I knew I could take part of it, if I wanted.

The Bogs had far more magic than either of us. We just had to figure out how to use it.

I took Mistral's hand, then placed his palm against the earth, laying my hand over his. I met his gray eyes solidly. "We're going to try."

"You care that much if he lives or dies?" He seemed almost shocked by the notion.

"He's not going to die. Now call up that wild magic. I know you're connected to it."

He continued watching me. "We barely controlled it before. If it overwhelms us, I will die, and you may end up coming with me."

I felt a flash of fear but I shoved it back down. The cut across my throat still stung. I had already faced death once this night—had barely evaded it. I looked down at Gabriel, his chest hardly rising and falling with breath. "Do it."

Mistral's hand flexed beneath mine, then I felt it, like a massive feral beast rising up beneath us. The magic of the land came to his call, wild, uncontrollable, and *hungry.*

I kissed him, and some of that magic jumped to me, searing through my veins like molten metal. With one hand still on the earth, he slid the other behind my neck, pulling my lips against his almost painfully. He fed at my mouth, passing the magic between us, making it unfurl inside my gut like a blooming rose.

Not knowing what I was doing, I gripped Gabriel's limp hand, his skin far too cold.

Mistral pulled back slightly, our lips still almost touching. Magic thrummed in my throat like a second heartbeat. "We must direct it. Before, we were only trying to contain it, to shove it back down."

My breathing grew ragged as the magic quickly overwhelmed me. What had I been thinking? Why did I think I could control this? Sweat beaded across my brow, stinging my eyes. "Tell me what to do," I rasped.

He kissed me again, more lightly this time, though I could tell he was teetering on the brink. The land's magic was entirely overwhelming, and I was only feeling a portion of it. He broke the kiss to say, "Close your eyes."

It was difficult to obey. I felt like if I closed them, everything was going to disappear. Him, Gabriel, and the ground beneath us. If I closed my eyes, that dark, hungry thing swarming upward would swallow me whole.

I squeezed Gabriel's limp hand and closed my eyes.

"If you fight it, it will destroy you."

His words were far too close to my thoughts. I needed to pull away. I needed to run. I—

Gabriel's hand spasmed in mine. That big, strong hand. He had protected me. He barely even knew me, not really. And yet, he had been willing to give his life tonight to keep the fae from chasing after me. He had wanted me to run, to leave him behind.

And that simply wasn't an option.

I took a deep breath, stilled my thoughts, pushed

down my fears, and I let the magic take over. I opened myself to it—because that's what it really wanted. An outlet. It was wild magic, and it had been kept under control for too long.

"Gabriel is a part of this land, Eva. Will the magic into him. Show it how to save him."

I shook my head in sharp, jerky movements. I could barely keep my thoughts straight, let alone control something so powerful. "Why can't you do it?" My words were so soft I wasn't sure he heard me.

Then, he answered, "I am a servant of this land, bound to it, but not its master. I maintain balance, nothing more. But you—you're celestial. You can shift the very stars. The fates themselves. Shift his fate, Eva."

Tears dripped down my hot cheeks. I felt something slithering over my leg, and fought every instinct I had to not pull away. I knew it was a vine. We couldn't hold the magic forever. We were going to lose control.

I had never hated my mom more than I did in that moment, for leaving me to figure things out on my own. For never teaching me. I had only known other night runners, most with less celestial blood than me. None of them could have prepared me for this. I cried as more vines started swarming over us.

I didn't know what to do. I didn't know how to fight it, let alone control it. The magic choked me, filled me up to bursting.

I could feel Mistral's resignation. He knew it wasn't going to work.

I finally opened my eyes, taking in the same resignation in his expression that I had already sensed. I looked down at Gabriel, who had gone far too still. I remembered him impossibly strong, pulling me up onto his horse, keeping me steady. I remembered our kiss, and how I had slunk away, embarrassed. But he never gave me a hard time over it.

I owed it to him to try.

Not knowing what I was doing, I pushed away the vines trying to crawl up my body. I leaned over Gabriel, pressing my lips against his.

He didn't move. He didn't breathe.

I opened myself further, letting every drop of wild magic flow through me. The vines snaked up my body faster. I kissed Gabriel, and I pushed all of that magic into him.

My mind became nothing but the pounding rhythm of the earth. To control such things, there was a price. There was always a price.

Then I felt Mistral's hands on my back, his touch returning me to myself, at least enough for me to think again. Enough for me to realize Gabriel's hands had lifted to my waist. He pulled me against him, deepening our kiss.

I was so relieved, more tears streamed from my closed eyes, but the magic was still there, wrapping around us. It had given us the gift of healing, and now we had to pay the price.

And I didn't know if it was the magic wrapped

tightly around us, or just too many near death experiences in one day.

But it was a price I was willing to pay.

19

My shirt and bra were gone in an instant, and I pressed my bare chest against Gabriel for the very first time, feeling all that hard muscle beneath me, warm and real and *alive*. His fingertips skimmed up my sides, then his arms wrapped around me, holding me against him.

"Eva." His muttered words sent a thrill straight to my core, his tone so different from what I usually experienced.

I sensed another presence at my back, then Mistral leaned over me, placing a gentle kiss on my neck. "I can try leaving you two alone, but if the magic becomes too difficult to control, I will have to intervene."

Gabriel's hands kneaded my lower back and I groaned, grinding my hips against him. I appreciated being given the option, but it didn't feel right sending Mistral away. He was a part of this. Part of all we had conjured up.

I lifted myself, hugging my knees around Gabriel's sides as I straddled him. I met his darkened gaze, a question on the tip of my tongue.

He nodded, saving me from speaking. "It's okay."

The vines had started snaking around us again, but this time I didn't care as Mistral moved close, kissing the pulse near my throat. Gabriel's large hands moved up my sides, then gripped my breasts.

My breath caught in my throat at the physical sensations coupled with the thrum of wild magic around us—*within* us. Gabriel sat up, his height putting us eye to eye. I lifted my hands from the tugging vines, cradling his jaw as I kissed him. His tongue slid over mine just as Mistral kissed my neck again, making my entire body pulse with heat. Just this—just their mouths on me as wild magic flowed through us—was almost too much.

Gabriel gripped my back, then spun me beneath him, placing me gently on the grass. The vines behaved themselves, cushioning me rather than restraining me. Gabriel kissed down my chest, then sucked my breast into his mouth, teasing my nipple with his tongue.

I tossed my head back, my senses overwhelmed with the scent of earth and grass, and beyond that the scents of the men I had come to know.

Gabriel's kisses moved further down my body. As he unbuttoned my jeans, Mistral moved toward us. He leaned on one elbow, stroking the hair out of my face with his free hand. "You're glowing, Eva."

And so I was. Around my hands pressed against the earth, tiny stars glittered. I stared at them, transfixed, then Gabriel tugged off my pants and underwear and found me with his mouth.

I threw my head back again, my eyes fluttering closed.

Mistral's lips skimmed my cheek. "When the time comes, we must be sure to send the magic back below."

I inhaled sharply as Gabriel found just the right spot with his tongue. "I don't know how," I panted.

"I will be here to help you." Mistral's hand found mine, our fingers twining. "Just like last time."

I squeezed his hand, the only answer I could give as the orgasm hit me. I could feel the heartbeat of the earth beneath us, pleased because I had relinquished my last shred of control. Sex was magic too. Energy. And the land thrived on it.

Gabriel's tongue slid across me a final time, then he lifted his head enough to lay his cheek on my abdomen. I moved my free hand to stroke my fingers through his dark hair. "Don't think you're getting off that easy," I panted.

He lifted his head enough to look at me, then seeing my expression, he smiled. "What exactly do you have in mind?"

Dropping Mistral's hand, I pushed Gabriel back until I could climb onto his lap, straddling him. I could feel the hard length of him through his pants, pressing against me. Just the small brush stole a gasp from my lips. The feel of magic around us had quieted, as if it was waiting to see what would happen. Tiny stars floated around us, casting hints of light on the night-darkened greenery.

I kissed Gabriel, remembering his hurt when I hadn't wanted to kiss him before. I never wanted to see him like that again. My arms locked around the back of his neck as he suddenly stood, taking me with him. One large hand cupped my bare ass as the other undid his pants, letting them fall to the ground. He lowered me just enough to feel that he either hadn't been wearing underwear, or they had gone with the pants.

I groaned, trying to lower myself further, wanting the press of him against me, but his hand held me steady. I heard the crinkle of foil and realized Mistral had handed him a condom. I would be eternally grateful for his clear-headedness, because the mixture of adrenaline and magic had me not thinking straight.

It was almost enough to bring me back to myself, to get embarrassed and question what I was doing, then Gabriel slipped the condom on and pressed against my opening.

"Oh gods," I panted.

He pressed further into me, going slow to make space. I should have known that such a large goblin would have such a large—

I tossed my head back, my breath sighing out of me. He held both my hips in his hands, sliding the rest of the way in before grinding me against him, then he lowered me to the ground.

The stars closed in as he looked down at me, slowly drawing himself out before thrusting in deeply. I pressed my fingers into the ground, digging through the grass to touch damp soil. He continued thrusting, another orgasm building in my core.

The magic around us seemed to build again at the same time, with tendrils of vines snaking around my body. Gabriel cried out just as another orgasm hit me, pounding into me with abandon as he came. I tried to remember what Mistral told me about the magic, that I needed to send it back below, but I found myself opening to it instead. Drawing it inside of me until the stars around us were almost too bright. Gabriel thrust into me one last time, then slumped over me, panting.

I ran my fingers through the soft hair across the back of his skull, forcing my eyes open. Mistral was there, looking down at us, clearly worried.

I opened my mouth to ask him what was wrong, then the earth trembled beneath us, like a sleeping giant had just turned over in his bed.

Gabriel sat up, taking me with him, keeping me protectively in his lap. "The magic."

"Yes. It must still be dealt with." Mistral moved closer, his eyes on me. "I apologize, but I might need to be more involved. Gabriel does not share the same connection to the land."

I licked my parted lips. "No apologies necessary." My voice came out breathy and he smiled.

I kissed Gabriel one last time, then crawled from his lap toward Mistral.

Mistral's brows rose at the sight of me, completely nude, crawling toward him. "My, you are a deadly little thing, aren't you?" His voice was just as breathy as mine had been.

"You have no idea." I pushed a hand against his chest as I reached him. The feel of the wild magic and the growing things all around us had me feeling almost feral. And I couldn't say that I disliked the sensation. It was nice letting go for once. Being entirely in my own skin.

I followed Mistral down with my hands, ending with my fingers on the button of his pants. I undressed him slowly, although the magic urged me to hurry. Once he was naked before me I took a moment to just look at him, his gray skin perfect atop the vibrant green grass and vines, his white hair strewn around him. A few vines snaked across him almost lovingly.

"The land cares for you," I said, not sure where the thought had come from.

"In its own way." He took one of my hands, pulling me down on top of him.

I lifted myself slightly as he slipped on a condom— thank the gods he was entirely prepared, though I'd have to ask him later why he was carrying *two* of them. For the moment though, I didn't care. He steadied himself with one hand as I slid down onto him, my eyes fluttering with pleasure at the sensation.

He gripped my hips until I opened my eyes and gave him my full attention.

"When the time comes—"

I nodded. "The magic is all yours."

He gave me a pleased smile, then lifted his hips, thrusting into me. It was all the incentive I needed. I rode him as living vines tickled my skin, and tiny stars danced around us. Just as I was nearing orgasm, Gabriel came around my side and kissed me. The magic built as I came, and I opened myself not only to it, but to Mistral. It flowed through us both back into the earth, entirely satisfied, and my tiny dancing stars went with it.

Gabriel braced me as my body went limp, then he gently laid me atop Mistral.

Mistral kissed the top of my head, holding me against him. "You could make a man wish to never go home, Eva," he muttered.

My heart welled at the thought of him going home, of leaving this realm forever, and of me helping him do it. But I forced the emotions back down. They would do me no good.

Gabriel curled onto his side next to us, putting an arm around me, his fingers skimming up and down my waist.

And together, with the taste of wild magic still coating our skin, we slept.

20

I woke in a tangle of vines and arms with soft sunlight warming my bare skin. I panicked for a moment until I remembered where I was, and that the arms around me were Mistral's and Gabriel's. And that last night—

Oh holy hells. I wasn't sure how I had gone from basically celibate, to this.

I tried to sit up, but vines and moss had formed a blanket over the lower halves of our bodies.

Chuckling, Mistral sat up beside me, helping me push the greenery away.

I glared at him. "I suppose this is just a regular morning for you, huh?"

His gray eyes sparkled in the sunlight, and his smile was the most genuine I had seen from him. "Not quite." He reached toward me, then pulled a leaf from my hair.

I sensed Gabriel sitting up behind me and glanced back at him. "And what about you?"

One corner of his grim mouth curled ever so slightly. "No. I try to not make nearly dying a regular event." His expression softened. "Although I cannot complain about being saved."

I looked at my watch—the only article still adorning my body—and groaned. Thirteen missed calls from Braxton. The others must have told him what happened.

I pushed the button to call him back, and we all waited in silence as it rang.

"In the name of all things good, bad, or whatever, Eva, what the hell took you so long to call me back?"

I winced, having no idea what to say. "I'm guessing someone told you what happened?"

"All I know is that Fae attacked the border and some psychopath drove by, shouting like a maniac for them to follow her. Then we found some bodies further down the road next to a freshly felled tree, dragged just far enough for a vehicle to get by."

I absorbed his words. That must have been Crispin and Elena. Sebastian probably popped out just as soon as I did. He wouldn't have cared about Ringo, but I hoped the elves would have taken him with them.

"Hellooooo? Care to tell me what's going on?"

I swiped a palm over my face. "It's an exceedingly long story, one better given in person. Were any wolves hurt?"

"A few injuries, but no one dead. I'm guessing your devil is just fine, but what about the others?"

I looked at Mistral, then Gabriel, my cheeks burning. "Fine as far as I know. Though I should probably check in with Elena."

Braxton sighed heavily. "You do that, then meet me at home. You owe me dinner."

"For what!"

"I don't know, but for some reason I feel like you owe me for something."

Considering I had brought the fae to his pack's doorstep, he was probably right. "I'll pick something up on my way back from Emerald Heights."

"Is it really safe for you to be walking around?"

"Probably not, but I need to figure a few things out." Like why Elena's father lied about the sword, and why Ivan had sent the fae after me when I was supposed to be protected.

"Watch your back, Eva. I'll see you at home."

He hung up, and I slumped limply back against the grass. Mistral and Gabriel both looked down at me with identical expressions.

"I'm going to Emerald Heights. I have to."

"It's not that," Mistral said. "I sense a devil waiting outside our boundary."

I covered my face with both palms and shook my head against the grass. "Please tell me my clothing survived the night."

My clothing had not survived the night. At least not entirely. My jeans were torn, but wearable. My shirt, not so much. We at least found both of my sneakers, and Mistral lent me his shirt.

I debated taking a detour to the Citadel to clean up before meeting Sebastian, but I didn't want him to get tired of waiting and leave.

Not that I wanted to see him, but I wasn't foolish enough to face the elf king alone. He'd invited Sebastian in once. He could do it again.

With no sinks or streams to be found, Mistral held my face, gently wiping a smudge of dirt from my cheek. His eyes were earnest as he said, "Thank you."

"Perhaps I should be the one thanking her," Gabriel's voice rumbled behind me.

I glance back to give him a wry look. "You were only injured because of me."

I hadn't had a chance to tell them what the fae told me the previous night, that my mother hadn't doomed everyone, that she had in fact saved them. I wasn't sure what to think of it, and given the person who'd told me had then attempted to slit my throat, I wasn't entirely inclined to believe him. But *he'd* believed it. He had believed it enough to want to kill me. And there might be others who thought the same.

Oddly, the person I most wanted to speak with about it was Sebastian. His thoughts wouldn't be clouded with the desire to keep me safe. He would do whatever needed to be done.

"What are you thinking?" Mistral asked.

I opened my mouth to say *nothing*, then realized it would technically be a lie. Instead, I just gave him a small smile and shook my head.

He took my hand to guide me to the path, perfectly comfortable without a shirt. And who could blame him? He looked *right* amongst the lush greenery, the sunlight shining softly on his stone gray skin, his long hair skimming his bare back.

Gabriel fell into step at my other side. He was also shirtless, because his clothing was torn and soaked with blood. I could see the dried stains of it on his pants, making my gut twist. He had come so close to dying, and the idea had pained me so much more than I ever thought it would.

I was getting attached. I knew I was getting far too attached not only to a goblin prince who hoped to return home, but to his loyal vassal, who I knew must be planning to go with him.

I needed to pull back, to gain some distance, but Mistral's hand felt far too nice in my own. And when he released it for Gabriel to lift me over a massive fallen log, butterflies erupted in my chest.

Gods, this was almost more dangerous than the fae trying to kill me.

By the time we reached the gates, the sun was high in the sky, and Sebastian was still waiting. Even with the dark lenses covering his eyes, I could read his bored expression. An act, I thought. Although, he was a devil.

Maybe it wasn't an act. Maybe the events of the previous day and night had not phased him at all.

His head turned in our direction as we approached. I wished I could see his eyes. I couldn't quite tell if he was looking at me, or the shirtless goblins on either side of me. Then my heart swelled as I noticed Ringo at his feet. The little goblin perked up at the sight of us.

I ran toward the gate, grinning as Ringo scurried over to meet me there. "Ringo! I'm so sorry I left you. I didn't mean to. I just—"

He was practically bouncing with excitement. "Sebastian let me ride on his shoulder!" He bit back his words, glancing warily at the devil.

"If only she was that excited to see either of us," Mistral mused.

I rolled my eyes, but didn't have time to reply as Sebastian approached. He removed his sunglasses, looking Gabriel up and down before turning to me. "It seems you had an interesting night."

I bit my lip. "Um. Yes. Where are Elena and Crispin?"

"Emerald Heights. I told them I would bring you as soon as I managed to locate you." He slid his sunglasses back into place. "Which is much easier when you actually carry your card."

I rolled my eyes again. "It doesn't work here anyway." And he knew exactly where to find me. He knew this is where I would bring Gabriel.

"Are you ready?"

My brows raised. I had really expected more questions. Or at least some mean remarks aimed toward my escorts. "Yeah, I guess I am." I looked down at Mistral's too large shirt and my stained and torn jeans. "But a shower and some fresh clothing would be nice."

"I will escort you."

Gabriel shifted beside me, ready to step forward, and I put a hand on his arm. "He's not going to let anything happen to me. The fae who attacked us are dead, and if more come, we're in the city now. The elves are watching."

"And the goblins," Mistral added.

Sebastian waited with his arms crossed, once again looking bored.

I hesitated with my hand still on Gabriel's arm. I really didn't want to do anything in front of Sebastian, but—

Last night had been our first night together. I wanted him to know it had meant something, something beyond just saving him. So I stood on my toes and planted a light kiss on his lips. Only the faintest hint of magic flared between us, as if it was still tired and satisfied from last night.

His eyes widened as I pulled away, then he smiled. "I'm here if you need me."

I smiled back, then looked at Mistral, worried he might be jealous. But he seemed genuinely happy. Glad that I cared enough to reassure his friend. And that... that meant something too.

Gods, what had I gotten myself into?

Sebastian opened the gate, and I shifted to step across the boundary. The shift came so effortlessly that I just stood there for a moment. I couldn't help but wonder if more had changed last night than just my relationship with Gabriel and Mistral.

I lifted Ringo to my shoulder, then looked back at the guys. "I'll let you know how it goes with King Francis."

Worry crossed both of their expressions, but they didn't try to stop me. They knew I had to go, and they couldn't come with me. Not unless we convinced King Francis to give Gabriel a free pass as well, but that would take time. And deep down, I felt like I had already asked for far too much.

"Shall we?" Sebastian asked.

I nodded, glancing back at the guys one last time as Sebastian led me away. We walked down the winding path, back toward the city in silence.

Then, just as we reached the street, Sebastian leaned in near my shoulder. "I believe I know who the fae was who tried to kill you last night. And I know why."

21

WE WAITED at the golden gates of Emerald Heights for Elena to arrive. Sebastian had escorted me to my apartment, and I now was freshly showered and wearing clean jeans, a lightweight blue flannel, and brown boots. I wiped my palms on my jeans again, shifting my weight nervously.

Sebastian had told Elena and Crispin the night before that he would find me and bring me here. Then, instead of waiting for me at the Bogs, he had paid Elizabeta, the vampire master of the city, a visit. Because if Ivan was still sending people after me, he was going directly against her orders, and her alliance with the elf king.

There he had learned one highly important piece of information. Ivan was dead, killed by Elizabeta herself for scheming behind her back.

That left one very important question. Who had

actually sent the fae?

Hopefully soon, all would be revealed.

I straightened as I spotted Elena approaching, once again riding the huge buck, with a second creature for Sebastian. She looked a little green around the edges, and I imagined too many beers, plus a battle to the death, followed by a car ride, wasn't good for anyone. Let alone an elven princess who likely hadn't seen many wild nights.

She climbed down from her buck, then opened one side of the golden gates, her oversized gray sweatshirt barely revealing her hands as she did so. Despite her disheveled state, she smiled at me. "Gods, am I glad to see you. When you disappeared like that, I wasn't sure what had happened. But this one assured me you would be fine." She nodded toward where Sebastian stood, arms crossed beneath the shade of a tree. "Is Gabriel..."

"He's fine."

Another relieved smile. Sebastian didn't think she was hiding anything from us, and I had to agree. Whatever schemes were afoot, Elena was not part of them. "You must truly be a miracle worker."

"It was an interesting night," I said vaguely. No way was I revealing everything that happened, at least not in front of Sebastian.

She reached into the pocket of her jeans and produced another small glass leaf. "Courtesy of my father, although after he got a look at me this morning, he did express concerns over my new... friends."

"Hey, you're the one who tried to out-drink a bunch of werewolves."

Sebastian approached, taking the offered leaf. "We would like to explain things to your father ourselves. Can you bring us to him?"

Her eyes shifted to me, and I gave her an encouraging nod.

"We should get going then. He should be just finishing up his daily game of chess with Zenith by the time we get there."

I assumed Zenith was the cranky companion I had met previously, but I didn't ask questions. I merely nodded, nervous about the events ahead.

"Eva will ride with me." Sebastian walked toward the second buck.

Elena lifted a brow at me, and I shrugged. We didn't think Elena was in on anything, but we couldn't be sure. Not that I thought she was going to push me off a moving animal, but Sebastian was being unusually paranoid after all he'd learned.

I followed Sebastian, feeling a little braver than before. If I took nothing else from my recent experiences, at least I was a lot more comfortable around large animals.

I looked up into the buck's glassy dark eye. I was a lot more comfortable, but that didn't mean I was any better at climbing on top of them. Before I could request a boost from Elena—I couldn't imagine Sebastian letting me step into his palm—Sebastian had his hands around my hips, propelling me upward.

I let out an embarrassing *yip* of surprise, landed across the buck's back on my stomach, then had to wiggle one leg over before I could sit upright. I blew my hair out of my face, then glared down at Sebastian.

"Really, you'd think you would be better at this by now."

My glare deepened. "Careful, or I'm going to ride this buck away from you and you can walk."

With a smirk, he used a low stump to vault up behind me, settling in far too close as he whispered, "Such animals don't obey terrified masters."

"I'm not terrified," I grumbled, then gripped his arm around me as the animal lurched into motion.

Elena's buck galloped beside us—did buck's gallop, or was that just horses?—then took the lead. Even at the high-speed, it would take a little while to get to the palace, so I settled in as comfortably as I could. But despite my best efforts I knew my butt was going to be bruised, and I was far too aware of Sebastian right behind me. My magic wasn't being called out, not yet, but it was still there just beneath the surface. His arm around me felt oddly intimate, and for some reason, I kept remembering him carrying me away from the fae he'd killed to save me.

A fae who was most certainly not what he seemed.

CRISPIN MET us as we arrived at the stable outside the palace. He looked fresh and rested in his crisp white button up, the top few buttons undone. Houndstooth slacks fit him perfectly, and his open waistcoat looked just right with the cobblestones and idyllic greenery. He jogged up beside our mount, plucking me from my place atop its back, then steadying me on the cobblestones.

I winced at the fresh pain in my backside. Elena must have buns of steel to ride around like this all the time.

Crispin looked at Elena as she dismounted, then over at Sebastian, then down at me. "Well? Is somebody going to tell me what happened? Did your giant goblin friend survive?"

"He's fine." I stepped away from him. We didn't think Crispin had lied to us either, but we couldn't be sure, not until we could confront the king.

It seemed a little foolish now, confronting him in his own palace, but Sebastian seemed confident we would survive.

"Then why do we all look so glum?"

Elena hurried past us, looking more green than glum. "Take them to see my father. I'm going to be sick."

Crispin watched her retreat around the corner with an eyebrow raised. "I did tell her all those beers would affect her differently than her father's honeysuckle wine."

I smiled. If I weren't so nervous, I might have

enjoyed seeing Elena at her worst. Not that I wanted her to suffer, but she seemed so formidable in every other aspect. Seeing her hungover made her more relatable.

Sebastian pressed a hand against the small of my back. "Shall we?"

Crispin bowed his head. "Of course. Though I don't know what you hope to learn. King Francis is a kind and honest man. Even if he knew of the—" he glanced around, then even though we were alone, finished, "*thing*, he surely had a good reason for keeping it to himself."

"We shall be the judge of that," Sebastian said tersely.

With a hesitant nod, Crispin gestured for us to walk through the nearest door.

As we walked down the long, sunny interior hall with greenery blooming brightly outside every window, my nerves kicked up another notch. Crispin glanced at me, almost as if he could sense it, but he didn't comment.

We found the king where we had expected, playing chess with his cranky friend Zenith. The king smiled at us, smoothing his hands down his blue embroidered coat. He looked a little older today, more tired, and I wondered if it was just worry over his daughter, or something more. We were about to find out.

Sebastian bowed slightly. "King Francis, I appreciate you allowing me into your lands."

The king's red brows rose. "Do not thank me yet. I hope you have a fine excuse for returning my daughter to me in such a condition."

I glanced back, realizing Crispin had remained by the door, clearly not part of the conversation. I watched him for a heartbeat longer, but he didn't meet my eyes.

"As you well know," Sebastian was saying, "Princess Millelena makes her own decisions."

The king chuckled, breaking some of the tension, and that only seemed to make his buddy Zenith crankier. He glared at me from beneath heavy blond brows, as if I were the true problem.

"May we speak in private?" Sebastian asked.

Zenith seethed at his words, but when the king gestured for him to step outside, he did so without complaint.

I felt a flash of Sebastian's dark magic, recognizing the sensation of him creating a bubble to keep out eaves-droppers.

The king narrowed his eyes for a moment, glancing over to Crispin, who nodded that it was okay.

"We know you were shown the Realm Breaker," Sebastian stated. "We know you were offered a chance at the bounty."

The king didn't react. He simply stared at Sebastian, *calculating*. "And what of it?" he finally asked.

"Do you not wish to be reunited with your true queen?"

The king's eyes flared. "Friend of my daughter's or not, I would warn you to choose your words wisely."

"An elf with powerful magic, glamoured to look like one of the fae, tried to kill Eva last night."

My pulse sped at his words, though he had already told me the truth. After I had taken off with Gabriel, Sebastian retreated to see if he could learn anything from the dead fae who had almost slit my throat. Only, he had been a fairy no longer. His death had dissolved the glamour.

The king's mouth fell open in genuine surprise.

I let out a heavy breath. He didn't know. He might have lied to his daughter about the blade, but he hadn't sent someone to kill me.

"Who? Who would disobey my direct orders?"

Sebastian pulled a printed photo out of his shirt pocket.

I caught a glimpse of it, and bile climbed up my throat. "You went back and took a *picture* of him?"

Sebastian's eyebrow twitched. "Would you rather I had brought the corpse for identification?"

At least now I knew Sebastian had been telling the truth. The corpse was an elf, looking vaguely like the man who'd tried to kill me.

The king's mouth formed a grim line as he studied the photo. He looked at it for a long while, then slowly shook his head. "That is Zenith's younger brother."

I inhaled sharply.

"And was Zenith present when you were shown the sword?" Sebastian asked.

"He was." The king's shoulders slumped. "But I cannot believe he would go so far." He pinched his brow and shook his head. "If I knew, I could have stopped this. I could have spared Kai's life."

Kai. The elf who'd tried to kill me. The king's grief was palpable. So intense that I almost felt bad about my would-be murderer's death.

"He said he wanted the pathways to remain closed," I said softly. "And I think you want the same."

He looked at me, reddish brows furrowed over tired eyes. "I thought in offering you my protection, and allowing you to be close to my daughter, I could keep an eye on things. I could keep anyone else from using you, and if you got too close on your own, I could then interfere."

"But why?" I asked. "Your daughter believes you would give anything to reunite with the one you love. Why would you want to prevent that from happening?"

"Because it is not safe. Even if we could reopen the pathways, the elves would stay far away from them. Not for what would happen to us, but for what would happen to our home. Our *true* home."

Crispin finally stepped forward. "What are you talking about?"

The king wilted further, like an invisible weight was crushing him. "I know why the pathways were destroyed. I know, because I helped make it happen."

22

Banging on the door had us all turning in that direction. Sebastian sighed, then I felt his magic retreat. The door flew open and Elena came staggering in.

"What in the hells was that? Why couldn't I enter? It was so quiet in here, I thought something terrible had happened."

"The devil was protecting the room," the king explained to his daughter. "But I suppose you should hear this as well. It's time for you to know the truth."

Elena glanced around at all of us. She was still a little pale, but looked better. Probably because she had been heaving her guts up.

The king looked at Sebastian. "If you don't mind?"

Sebastian nodded, then walked past Elena to shut the door behind her. A moment later, I felt another flash of his magic.

The king looked again at his daughter. "Come, Millelena. Sit. I know you are not feeling... well."

"What's going on, father?"

He sighed heavily. "The myths about the Realm Breaker are all true. It was used to sever the pathways, but it was not just a lone celestial who wielded it. She never could have done it on her own." He gave me a meaningful look. "Each of us, the leaders of our people, were shown the truth. And we helped her sever each of our pathways."

"What truth?" I asked. Whatever it was, the man who had attacked me last night knew something of it. He knew why the pathways were destroyed.

"The truth was that in coming here, we doomed our home realms. We stole magic away, and left an open door behind us for anyone else to come in." He looked at each of us. "It is not just earth and our realms that exist. There are other things out there. Dark and dangerous things. They were just starting to slip through, but it would have gotten worse. So much worse. The celestials saw it first, and created the sword. But each of us had to agree. We had to give up our pathways. And we had to remain here, trapped. There was no time to gather our people, and we could not abandon them."

Elena stepped forward, standing between me and Crispin. "It cannot be true. You could not keep such a thing secret."

He gave her a sad look. "Would you have had me

admit to my people that I trapped them here? We all agreed that no one else must know. It was the only way to keep everyone safe."

My mind raced. I didn't know much about what happened beyond some of the boundaries, but the goblins... Mistral's mother had kept the Bogs under control when she was still alive. Had she too agreed that the pathways should be destroyed? And had she kept it from her own son? There was no way he could know. With our bargain of truth, it would have come out by now.

The king looked at me. "Zenith knows the truth. He was there, and it seems he told his younger brother. For that, I am sorry. I wish he would have trusted me to keep it under control."

Seemingly stunned, Crispin finally stepped forward. "I didn't see anything dark or terrible when I came here."

"Because you created a fresh pathway," the king grumbled. "I was terrified when you first arrived, but then you were trapped here yourself. Whatever pathway you forged, it was temporary. And here, you do not have enough power to forge another. At least not all the way to our homeland."

I rubbed at my temple, fighting a headache. If my mother really was the one to wield the Realm Breaker, and if everything the king had said was true, the man who tried to kill me was right. She had *saved* everyone. Then, with everyone agreeing to keep what they did a secret, she went into hiding. But eventually, someone found out. Someone blamed the celestials for destroying the pathways. And that had been when she left and took all my memories with her. Which meant...

"I knew."

The king's brows lifted and I shook my head, since I wasn't really speaking to him. "I knew. I knew something about what happened, and that's why my mother took my memories."

Elena and Crispin both gave me stunned looks. With all the new information, I had actually forgotten that they didn't know. But I supposed there was no point in keeping it a secret now.

"That's why I'm trying to find her," I explained. "When she left, she took my memories. There was so much I lost of her, my childhood... of my father. I wanted them back. I *want* them back. But now I understand why she took them. She had to make sure I didn't know anything. It would have put me exactly in the situation I'm in now, only it would've happened when I was just ten years old."

Stunned silence surrounded me, until finally, Sebastian cleared his throat. "Regardless of what has happened, the bounty still exists. The Realm Breaker is still up for grabs. And those who want it will not stop." He looked at me. "You will never be safe until all of this is over."

I blinked at him. "But now we know the pathways

were closed for a reason. What happens if we reopen them?"

The king stood abruptly. "Did you not just hear what I told you? They must not be reopened. I sacrificed *everything* to protect my people. I will not have that sacrifice be in vain."

I flinched at his sudden anger, realizing that maybe he was starting to agree with Zenith. Maybe it would be easier for him if I was dead.

Sebastian was suddenly closer, gripping my shoulder. "The fae were not sent after Eva by Ivan. They were sent by you."

My heart skipped a beat. We knew about Kai, but the fae—

The king pressed a palm to his forehead and shook his head. "I only hoped to frighten you. I did not know that Zenith would send his younger brother with them." He lifted his head and met my eyes. "I am not so blind to ignore the hypocrisy in taking an innocent life to protect others. I only wanted to sway you from your path, not harm you." He looked at Elena. "And I did not expect you to get so deeply involved."

"The fae stabbed my friend with a poisoned blade." I stepped toward the king without thinking, pulling away from Sebastian. "They weren't just trying to frighten us."

His expression turned stony. "I was not aware of that." He glanced at his daughter again. "And had I realized Elena's intentions, I would have planned differently." His eyes drifted back to me. "I did not believe you would be so difficult to apprehend. They were to put a fright into you, then allow you to escape. I imagine once they feared for their lives, they were willing to kill to save themselves." He looked again at his daughter, both tired, and maybe irritated that she had been keeping things from him.

"She was trying to help you," I said. "She wanted to reunite you with someone you lost, and I know that has to be the case for so many others, you all live so damn long." I thought of Mistral, but kept my mouth shut. He didn't just want to return home because he missed it. He couldn't maintain the Bogs forever, and too many of the goblins wouldn't survive without their realm.

I caught Sebastian watching me, and knew he must've realized what I was thinking, because he smiled, the bastard. He knew that despite the king's warning, and despite what had almost happened, I couldn't give up, and not just for myself.

"Eva is right." Elena stood a little straighter, looking a lot more confident than I felt. "Whatever the darkness was in the pathways, it will have to be dealt with. We can't just give up."

The king sighed heavily. "You don't understand what you're saying."

She lifted her chin. "That doesn't make me any less right. Perhaps I should have been upfront with you. Perhaps the altercation with the fae could have been avoided. *But*," she lifted a finger, "I'm still right."

The king's cheeks reddened at his daughter's tone. "You do not understand, Millelena. There is too much at risk."

Elena's eyes flared, and she opened her mouth to argue, but Crispin cleared his throat, stepping forward. "If I may intervene, there is perhaps another way."

Everyone looked at him, and I had to admit, I admired the way he didn't wilt under so many heavy gazes. He looked at the king. "You said nothing came through with me because I created my own pathway, and I believe you are correct. I came through what equated to an ant's tunnel, when the former pathways were like giant ravines. It is possible that with the Realm Breaker, we can create more such tiny tunnels. Or just one, an exploratory mission to see what we find on the other side." He looked at me. "Of course, this is all dependent on Eva finding her mother. Which she will have to do *without* the sword. But judging by the progress she has already made, I think she can do it. I think with practice she could create a pathway small enough just for her, leading to her mother."

"Or to the person with the Realm Breaker," Elena added.

I noticed the king watching me intently, and fought the urge to squirm. He lowered his chin. "This is all dependent on the assumption that Eva would give us the sword once she has it," he said. "If I had it here, safe beyond our boundary, the hunt for her would end." His eyes flicked to Sebastian. "But I'm guessing she has other... obligations."

I winced, wondering if Sebastian was *ever* going to step into the conversation. I looked at him expectantly.

He simply smiled, entirely unruffled. "While Eva is obligated to provide me with either the sword or her mother, I will not require the use of the blade indefinitely." He looked at the king. "If you are willing to help us now, I believe a mutually beneficial compromise can be struck."

The king narrowed his eyes at the devil. "We will need to speak further to hammer out the terms, *if* such a bargain is to be struck."

Sebastian nodded.

"Okay, so it's settled," I said, "We work together. But I have one extra term of my own."

Everyone looked at me. "The goblins get to use the blade too."

"One goblin," the king countered. "One goblin may go on—" he looked at Crispin, "what did you call it?"

"An exploratory mission."

"Yes," the king continued, turning his attention back to Sebastian. "Is this amenable to you?"

But Sebastian was still watching me, a smile on his face and a telltale flash of fire in his eyes. "*One* goblin," he agreed.

I could almost *hear* all the strings attached to the offer, but it was better than I'd hoped to get. I could try to help Mistral *and* I could fulfill my contract.

"Now," Sebastian continued before I could say anything else. "What of the elf who tried to have Eva killed?"

Elena gasped, then turned wide eyes to me. "What exactly did I miss?"

Epilogue

I WAITED with Crispin in his tower while the king and Sebastian negotiated their contract. Elena had gone to lie down. Crispin had placed a wooden chair next to the nicer cushioned chair near the window, offering me the better seat. His mood was surprisingly somber, given all of the excitement.

Finished preparing a pot of tea with a burner on his workstation, he poured us each a cup, offering me the one with fewer chips. "I must admit, out of all the scenarios I could have imagined for this day, I could not have come up with any of this."

I nodded, gripping the small teacup by its thin porcelain handle. The tea was strong and black, which was exactly what I needed. I couldn't quite meet his eyes as I asked, "Do you really think I can do it? Find my mother?"

He lowered himself to the seat beside mine. "I do,

especially if she is in one of the near realms, which she should be since she no longer possesses the Realm Breaker. The trick will be in figuring out *which* near realm."

"I can sense her when she's close," I admitted. "If we get close enough, I can find her." I saw him looking at me in my peripheral vision, but kept my eyes lowered, blowing the steam away from my cup.

"How old were you when she stole your memories?"

I tensed at his question.

"If you'd rather not say, that's fine."

"I was ten. My father died three years later." And he had paid a fairy to fake my death for my mother's benefit.

When he said nothing else, I finally looked at him.

He gave me a small smile. "If it helps, my father tried to kill me, and my mother sold me into apprentice-ship with a mad wizard."

My brows shot up at his words. I let out a choked laugh. "Seriously?"

He grinned. "See, you're not the only one with a complicated past."

I laughed again, shaking my head. "No," I said, thinking of Mistral, "I think compared to the lot of you, my past is boring in comparison."

"A fine way to look at it." Setting his tea aside, he stood and offered me his hand. "Now shall we?"

I stared dubiously at the offered hand. "Shall we, *what*?"

"If there's one thing I know, it's that old men take forever to hammer out contracts. We may as well make the most of our time and further explore your blossoming magic."

I nearly choked on my tea at Crispin calling Sebastian an old man, though technically, he was right. Relatively speaking, at least.

I set my tea aside, then hesitantly took Crispin's hand.

Once I was standing, he held on tight, standing a little too close, his eyes intense. "Now tell me, what exactly have you been doing in the Bogs to make your magic a little different every time I see you?"

I blinked at him, jaw agape.

"Don't worry, I can only see it because of my own innate magic. Elena hasn't noticed a thing."

I shut my jaw with a click. "If you want to know about *that*, I'm going to have to get to know you a hell of a lot better."

He grinned, still holding my hand. "Well, lovely Eva, there is no time like the present."

Also by Sara C. Roethle

A Study in Shadows

Hunters of the Helius Order have a single mission—track vampires, and kill them. Lyssandra lived her life by this purpose, until the day a vampire saved her from certain death. Now she is unwillingly bonded to him, a secret that will see her executed if her order learns the truth.

When she finds Asher, she'll cut out his heart for tying her to him, even if it kills her too. But when a young girl is found dead, Lyssandra's mission is derailed. In the gaping hole where the girl's heart once was, lies a single red rose. Lyssandra has seen the signature before, left by the vampire who took her uncle's life.

Karpov is one of the ancients, and his death is the only one Lyssandra wants more than Asher's. Unfortunately, Karpov is also the only being—dead or undead—who holds the key to Asher's whereabouts. If Lyssandra ever wants to find him, she'll have to work with her uncle's murderer.

Asher's death could finally bring her peace, but can she accept it when it means leaving her uncle's killer alive? Or will she fall into her master's waiting arms, unable to fight the pull of the unbreakable bond between them . . .

Books in the series:

Reign of Night
Blade of Demons
Heir of Shadow
Blood of Ancients

Tree of Ages

Finn doesn't know what—or who—uprooted her from her peaceful tree form, changing her into this clumsy, disconnected human body. All she knows is she is cold and alone until Àed, a kindly old conjurer, takes her in.

By the warmth of Àed's hearth fire, vague memories from her distant past flash across her mind, sparking a restless desire to find out who she is and what powerful magic held her in thrall for over a century.

As Finn takes to the road, she and Àed accumulate a ragtag band of traveling companions. Historians, scholars, thieves in disguise, and Iseult, a mercenary of few words whose silent stare seems to pierce through all of Finn's defenses.

The dangers encountered unleash a wild magic Finn never knew she possessed, but dark forces are gathering, hunting for Finn and the memories locked away in her mind. Before it's over, she will discover which poses the greater danger: the bounty on her head, or a memory that could cost her everything.

Books in the Series:
Tree of Ages
The Melted Sea
The Blood Forest
Queen of Wands
The Oaken Throne
Dawn of Magic: Forest of Embers
Dawn of Magic: Sea of Flames
Dawn of Magic: City of Ashes

The Moonstone Chronicles

The Empire rules with an iron fist. The Valeroot elves have barely managed to survive, but at least they're not Arthali witches like Elmerah. Her people were exiled long ago. Just a child at the time, her only choice was to flee her homeland, or remain among those who'd betrayed their own kind. She was resigned to living out her solitary life in a swamp until pirates kidnap her and throw her in with their other captives, young women destined to be sold into slavery.

With the help of an elven priestess, Elmerah teaches the pirates what happens to men who cross Arthali witches, but she's too late to avoid docking near the Capital. While her only goal is to run far from the political intrigue taking place within, she finds herself pulled mercilessly into a plot to overthrow the Empire, and to save the elven races from meeting a bloody end.

Elmerah will learn of a dark magical threat, and will have to face the thing she fears most: the duplicitous older sister she left behind, far from their home in Shadowmarsh.

Books in the series:
The Witch of Shadowmarsh
Curse of the Akkeri
The Elven Apostate
Empire of Demons
Legend of the Arthali
Gods of Twilight

Twilight Hollow Cozy Mysteries

An inept witch, a cozy town, and an old dark magic.

Welcome to Twilight Hollow, WA, a small forest town with three resident witches. Adelaide O'Shea runs the Toasty Bean, imbuing her coffee and tea with warm, cozy magic. When a black cat crosses her path, she worries her new pet might be unlucky, and her suspicions are confirmed when the next thing in her path is a dead man with her phone number in his pocket.

And the cops aren't the only ones breathing down her neck over it. There's an old, dark magic in town, and it has its sights set on Addy. With the help of her two witch sisters, a handsome detective, and a charming veterinarian, can Addy solve the murder and escape the darkness? Or will she and her new spooky pet have to turn tail and run?

Books in the Series:
Familiar Spirits
Catnip Cantrips
Tricky Treating
Feline Charm
Hideaway Hexes
Kitty Coven
Haunted Hijinks
Purrfect Crimes

The Thief's Apprentice

The clock ticks for London…

Liliana is trapped alone in the dark. Her father is dead, and London is very far away. If only she hadn't been locked up in her room, reading a book she wasn't allowed to read, she might have been able to stop her father's killer. Now he's lying dead in the next room, and there's nothing she can do to bring him back.

Arhyen is the self-declared finest thief in London. His mission was simple. Steal a journal from Fairfax Breckinridge, the greatest alchemist of the time. He hadn't expected to find Fairfax himself, with a dagger in his back. Nor had he expected the alchemist's automaton daughter, who claims to have a soul. Suddenly entrenched in a mystery too great to fully comprehend,

Arhyen and Liliana must rely on the help of a wayward detective, and a mysterious masked man, to piece together the clues laid before them. Will they uncover the true source of Liliana's soul in time, or will London plunge into a dark age of nefarious technology, where only the scientific will survive?

Books in the series:
Clockwork Alchemist
Clocks and Daggers
Under Clock and Key

The Will of Yggdrasil

The first time Maddy accidentally killed someone, she passed it off as a freak accident. The second time, a coincidence. But when she's kidnapped and taken to an underground realm where corpses reanimate on their own, she can no longer ignore her dark gift.

The first person she recognizes in this horrifying realm is her old social worker from the foster system, Sophie, but something's not right. She hasn't aged a day. And Sophie's brother, Alaric, has fangs and moves with liquid feline grace. A normal person would run screaming into the night, but there's something about Alaric that draws Maddy in.

Together, they must search for an elusive magical charm, a remnant of the gods themselves. Maddy doesn't know if she can trust Alaric with her life, but with the entire fate of humanity hanging in the balance, she has no choice.

Books in the series:

Fated

Fallen

Fury

Forged

Found

www.ingramcontent.com/pod-product-compliance
Lightning Source LLC
Chambersburg PA
CBHW030000010826

48973CB00007B/2100